LAST DAYS

by Brian Evenson

U

UNDERLAND PRESS
www.underlandpress.com
Portland, Oregon

Underland Press
www.underlandpress.com
Portland, Oregon

Cover image copyright © Karim Ghahwagi and Brian Evenson, 2007
Cover imaged used with permission from Karim Ghahwagi
Cover design by Heidi Whitcomb
Book design by Heidi Whitcomb

ISBN 978-0-9802260-0-3

Printed in the United States of America
Distributed by PGW

First Underland Press Edition: February 2009

10 9 8 7 6 5 4 3 2 1

For Paul

TABLE OF CONTENTS

INTRODUCTION

What Are You Doing, Where Are You Going, Who Are You?:
by Peter Straub

The first persons to mention the work of Brian Evenson to me were students in the Writing Division of the Columbia MFA program. Despite the handicap of never having taken or previously taught a course in creative writing, once a week during the month of October 2004, I conducted what Columbia called a "Master Class." In our first class session, not long after I learned that the campus bookstore had not yet received the students' copies of our text, I asked the fifteen people arrayed before me to name the writers they most admired, and boom, there it was, a whole new world. George Saunders, Jim Shepherd, Ken Kalfus, Gary Lutz, Brian Evenson, two or three others . . . Of the writers they mentioned, I knew the work of only Mary Caponegro, Lydia Davis, and Ben Marcus, the director of Columbia's writing program. Over the next few days, I ordered a good number of books by these writers, among them Evenson's *Altmann's Tongue*. Soon the books arrived and I read them, or at least started reading them, at least sampled them. Some of the stories in the books Amazon faithful delivered to my doorstep really worked, I thought, really made the case for their author's vision by maneuvering language and the old tools of character, situation, rhythm, and presentation into brilliant combinations and patterns. Some others seemed less successful, and a very few clearly had been written for an audience that did not include me. (Their resolute bad temper as prose narratives closed the door, but these same stories struck me as extremely interesting, even beautiful, if read as poetry. Apparently, a radical reinterpretation of basic genre markers had been put into play utterly without my noticing it. In the intervening four years, I came across examples of this process I found more congenial, chief among them being Rosalind Palermo Stephenson's great story, "Insect Dreams.")

Evenson and *Altmann's Tongue*, though, seemed to me to operate on another level altogether. In these stories, stoniness, obduracy, harshness, madness, and violence take wing and fly, released into the air by a completely original imagination. The early Evenson stories tend to stop you in your tracks with flat, declarative reports of monstrosity. Bodies litter the ground. Murders take place, again and again. A man chews his way out of his coffin. A man named Horst advises our unnamed first-person narrator to eat the tongue of Altmann, whom the narrator has killed, whereupon the narrator kills Horst, admires his handiwork, and (I think) turns into a crow. Former concentration camp barbers hang out together. Alfred Jarry and Ernst Jünger pop in and do things that might as well be called inscrutable. In a great story called "Two Brothers," a dying religious fanatic attempts to amputate his own gangrenous leg, but is murdered by one of his two sons, who cuts his eyes out of his head. Despite all the violence, which is somehow muffled by Evenson's spectacularly matter-of-fact delivery, the feel of the comic is never distant from the enterprise. It is not entirely clear where the comedy lies, unless it is in the extravagance of the grotesquerie. Very little else can be said to be extravagant.

In fact, an incredible amount is left out of these stories' rather sketchy narratives—landscapes, contexts in general, back stories, and history in general. The stories take place in a barren world that offers very little of the unspoken consolation provided by fictions in which the reader sees the characters park their (brand name and dashboard description supplied) cars, walk up their paths past the pansies and daffodils, open the fridge and take out a (brand name supplied) beer, then walk past a coffee table and a corduroy sofa to flop down onto a Barcalounger and point the remote at the TV. None of that ever happens in Evenson's fiction, unless the fridge contains a severed head and the corduroy is sticky with blood. The landscape inhabited by these Therons and Aurels and displaced writers is as stripped of particulars as the empty universe in which lovelorn Ignatz the mouse aimed bricks at the head of Krazy Kat. We might as well be in a desert. Also absent are the different, more profound consolations given by traditional narrative methods that establish tacit ground rules and expectations. Evenson was never at all interested in writing fiction that provided its own safety net. Without ever quite recognizing this habit, we enter fiction looking for the proscenium and the parted curtain, and when these comforting signs have been utterly erased, we readers have to deal with what turns out to be a productive anxiety. What does it say, to have violent acts depicted in such a thorough isolation, with such an absence of emotional affect? I don't mean "say" in some vaguely philosophical sense; I mean: what does it "say" to the *reader*? One has the sense of a requirement without much specificity as to the required. This in itself evokes a powerful requirement, that of suspending judgment, of maintaining openness to whatever thoughts are evoked in the reading process.

Before we move on to the book at hand, one other point should be made about Evenson's early, very striking fiction, namely that it clearly is the work of a writer just coming into his stride. Despite a pervasive nihilistic despair, the atmosphere and flavor of youth penetrate everything. This writer is willing to try almost anything that occurs to him, as long as it falls more or less within the circle of his aesthetics. Going wild makes him feel good, and he believes that when they read the results other people will feel good, too. Experiments with compression and duration tempt him. There are passages in these stories that, no matter how seriously their author took them, how much he understood to be at stake at even the simplest word-to-word level, undoubtedly made him laugh out loud with pleasure.

Throughout stories published over the six or seven years that followed *Altmann's Tongue*, as well as in the more mature and developed work Evenson has been producing since *Dark Property* of 2002, he has been demonstrating, illustrating, and justifying a consistent faith in the operations of the kinds of extremity present in his work from the beginning. *The Open Curtain*, published in 2006, uses a character's psychic disorder to push the novel into actual red-eyed, hell-for-leather narrative extremity, the only occasion I have ever seen in which a novel stops in its track and hunkers down to question its most elemental components. It's beautiful. It's stunning. It takes your breath away. The moment I read it, I knew that I had to steal it, and so I did, in the novel now sprawled out on my workbench/operating table, its little heart struggling to beat while its guts squirm beneath the editorial screwdrivers.

Extremity radiates through every inch of *Last Days*, though you would never know it from the book's odd, deliberate tone. This is a novel made of two novellas joined at the hip, where they share a common seam. When one ends, the other begins, and we are within a new fictional body, one that perfectly remembers all that took place in the body we just left. The narrative manner picks up with exactly the same gestures, i.e., minimal to none, and the same intention, to import into the Evensonian world a version of the hard-boiled detective novel, that its genre-specific stances, devices, and expectations might be upended, ignored, denied, and mocked with the straightest of faces.

With its traditional concerns for the restoration of order and proper assignment of blame, its well-nigh universal depiction of its detective-protagonists as agents of reason, personal honor, and proper communal ethics as represented by the marginalized, the detective novel makes an odd vessel for representation of extreme acts and extreme psychic states. In perhaps the greatest and most probing of all PI novels, Raymond Chandler's *The Long Goodbye*, the only psychic extremity on view—apart from Philip Marlowe's accelerating loneliness and disgust—is the product of his frequent beatings and consequent spells of unconsciousness. You would have to go to one-off eccentrics like Harry Stephen Keeler and John Franklin Bardin to find in detective fiction anything faintly comparable to the unflinching oddness, morbidity, and perversity of Brian Evenson in full spate, as in *Last Days*.

The novel begins with an after-the-fact recognition that, as far as our protagonist is concerned, everything was lost right from the beginning. It's pretty striking, this first sentence: *It was only later that he realized the reason they had called him, but by that time it was too late for the information to do him any good.* ". . . only later . . . too late . . ." The repetition lets us know that we really are in the Last Days, which begin at the very moment when it has become too late for intervention. In the Last Days, the apocalyptic circumstances gathering around us can no longer be reversed: don't start looking around for that Bible now, sorry, it's too late for herpicide. It is precisely this situation in which Evenson's detective, "Mr. Kline," more a non-hero or un-hero than hero or anti-hero, finds himself enmeshed in the novel's first few paragraphs.

Reluctant detectives, PIs who take cases on despite the feeling that they cannot end well, are far from uncommon in the mystery genre, but Kline takes this initial hesitation to its logical limit. Like most ruthlessly logical end-points, it turns out to be savagely irrational. He flatly refuses, a number of times, the job his callers are offering to him. He has two reasons for his refusals. Most days, Kline is too depressed to get out of bed. There is an excellent reason for his depression, namely that his left hand was severed by a foe, "the gentleman with a cleaver," who watched stunned as Kline cauterized his stump on a hotplate before shooting him in the eye. The depression occupies the precise amount of time it takes him to adjust to his traumatic loss.

The second reason Kline refuses the offer of a job is that he in no way needs the money. On his way out of the room he snaffled up several hundred thousand dollars. Not only does he not see taking the money as an act of theft, he regards it as "a profoundly moral act in a kind of moral, biblical, old testament sense: an eye for a hand, and a bag of money thrown in." Being without forgiveness or mercy, utterly cold-hearted and completely without nuance, and steeped in a code of well-earned retaliation, this version of the moral life far outdoes the simple desire for justice and clarity that animates most fictional private detectives. PIs like Marlowe and Lew Archer seek a kind of historical understanding, familial and societal, of the various messes wished upon them by their clients; as far as we can see, Kline is incapable even of conceiving of, much less desiring, such an understanding.

In his case, the familiar reluctance to take up a matter that seems too complex, too simple, or too draining to be rewarding is replaced by the detective's outright and obstinate refusal. In the end, his callers, Ramse and Gous, both of whom are at least as mutilated as he, must drag him out of bed, stuff him into a car, and deliver him to the man who set them in motion, Borchert. At every opportunity, Kline tells his captors that he wants out, he wants to go home. They want him to investigate a great crime, the murder of their founder and Borchert's only superior, Aline. Kline informs Borchert that he wishes to go home, but basically by persuading him to listen to a few of the details, Borchert gets him involved in the case. And then, protest though he does, he is involved, enmeshed. Much later in the story, Kline's request to go home has been replaced by the frequently voiced desire never to be bothered again by these lunatic people, and Paul—the prime figure in a competing band of lunatics, the Pauls— informs him that to be left alone, all he must do is kill every member of the Gous-Ramse-Borchert faction. And so far into blood and madness has he wandered that he agrees to commit mass murder. In the second half of this novel, Kline does very little else but murder people: the section "Last Days" accumulates a great many sentences that end with variations on the phrase, "and then he killed him with the cleaver." By Kline's hand, nearly everyone in the Borchert faction and the Pauls perishes; a severed head, Borchert's, has been dropped into a bucket and set on fire; behind the locked door of a burning building, the few who would have survived Kline's bloody progress through their world wind up screaming for help. This is where strict adherence to logic gets you.

Along the way, the plot and, often, the nature of the dialogue warp this insanely grim progress into pure dizziness. Betrayals are common elements in crime novels, so about halfway through "The Brotherhood of Mutilation," Kline is subjected to a gigantic, central betrayal that is echoed by a series of smaller treacheries that spin off into yet more minor yet still homicidal betrayals between secondary or even tertiary characters. As this pattern suggests, repetition of events both large and small forms the spine of this book. Sometimes the repetition is a mirroring, sometimes it plays out as an inversion. If early in the book Kline is surprised to discover Ramse and Gous in his apartment, late in the book he will find Gous cowering there: the act of self-mutilation that brings everything in its wake is echoed, at the midway point of the book, by another greatly like it. This constant ticking away of rhyming events often fades back into the swirl of outrageousness, improbability, and brutality that accompanies Kline as he is dragged back and forth between the opposing camps, but when we are reminded again of its presence, the awareness of frequent rhymes has a formalizing effect. We cannot take these murders and dismemberments at face value, for they have in effect been set to music.

In *Last Days*, people tend to speak in short, urgent bursts. They favor the single-sentence paragraph. This tendency evokes two contradictory modes, the hard-boiled and the comic, which inevitably ends with the comic tone undermining the echoes of Philip Marlowe and Mike Hammer. Here is a bit of dialogue with a drunken Ramse and Gouse and their bartender:

> "Ramse," said Kline. "Trust me and listen."
>
> Ramse opened his mouth, then closed it again.
>
> "Aline is dead," Kline said.
>
> "Aline is dead?" said Ramse, his voice rising.
>
> "Is that possible?" said Gous. "How is that possible?"
>
> "Or not," said Kline. "Maybe not."
>
> "Well," said Gous. "Which is it?"
>
> "What did you say about Aline?" asked the bartender.
>
> "Nothing," said Kline.
>
> "Oh, God," said Ramse, shaking his head. "Dear God."
>
> "Aline is either alive or dead," said Gous to the bartender.
>
> "Be quiet, Gous," said Kline.
>
> "Well, which is he?" asked the bartender. "There's a big difference, you know."

This knockabout minimalist ping-pong reminds me of Hemingway, but far more of Samuel Beckett, Harold Pinter, and even Joe Orton and David Mamet. It also seems deliberately to refer back to the Marx Brothers and the way the patter of 1930s vaudeville and burlesque comedians was represented in the 1950s by survivors like Bert Lahr and Ed Wynne, also by comedic teams like Abbot and Costello. We are not far from "The party of the first part" and "Who's on first?"

And let me just say this: cliff-hanger chapter endings, beautifully executed. It's like watching a magician snatch away a tablecloth without disturbing a formal, full-dress setting for eight.

This comedy, submerged but fully present, serves as an abiding corrective to the gravity of *Last Day*'s actual theme, which concerns the fanatical belief-systems and zealotry encouraged by some organized religions. The "mutilates" who thrust unwilling Kline into contact with their fellows count their spiritual progress in the number of joints, digits, eyes, tongues, and limbs they have amputated. Having (initially) lost only a hand, Kline would be a lowly, standard-issue one, but for the respect he generated by cauterizing his own stump. For a time, it seems that self-cauterization may become a fad amongst the mutilates. Schisms, most earnestly to be avoided, threaten to destroy a hard-won accord. The faithful are as prone to valorized acts of self-injury as high-school girls, and any extra suffering means another step closer to the divine. According to the original Paul, leader of the Pauls, he and the other two founders, the church fathers, were inspired by the admonition in Mark 9:43 to have a go at cutting off an offending hand, and understood immediately that they were on to something big. While Paul felt that a single act of mutilation satisfied the demands of the sacred realm, the others, Borchert and Aline, embarked on the course that led the Brotherhood to its present system of validation. (Aline, the most validated, therefore holiest and official spokesman of the group, is little more than a whittled torso and an eyeless, earless, noseless, tongueless cranium.) All of the bloodshed in the book flows from this original doctrinal schism—the men most prominent in this religion are those most prone to treachery and homicide.

Evenson's detective witnesses and takes part in all kinds of the childish mumbo-jumbo new faiths and other fraternal organizations employ to set themselves apart, inspire loyalty, and guarantee security for the faithful brotherhood. In varying degree, fraternal organizations from Skull & Bones to the Raccoon Lodge ritualize the appearance and observances of their membership. Some groups have actual uniforms, others content themselves with shared choices that add up to an ad hoc uniform. Have you seen Scientologists on the march in their Florida redoubt, members of the New York Athletic Club marching into their mansion on Central Park South, or Shriners whooping it up in a convention hotel? They don't really dress like other people, they dress like themselves. Ramse and Gous make Kline put on gray trousers, a white shirt, and (a brilliant detail) a red clip-on tie. That's what they all wear, the uniform of the anonymous white American drudge. Kline takes this fact in for a moment, then forgets it. So does the reader. The point of the uniform is that it is instantly forgotten.

Before the detective can be introduced to Borchert, certain ritual satisfactions must be accomplished at the gate. It is the guard's duty to enquire, "What is wanted?" and the applicant's duty to respond with the self-congratulatory formula, "Having been faithful in all things, we come to see he who is even more faithful than we." This rubbish sounds at least faintly parodic, but it is utterly surpassed by the formulaic rigmarole that goes on in the fortress of the Pauls, where the individuation of given names is erased and every remark of a person of higher status must be examined to determine if it is an orphic or parabolic bit of higher learning, a "teaching."

"What's your name?" Kline asked.

"I'm Paul," said the man.

"You're not," said Kline.

"We all are," he said.

Kline shook his head. "You can't all be Paul," he said.

"Why not?" said the man. "Is this a teaching?"

"A teaching?" Kline said. "What's that supposed to mean?"

"Should I write it down?"

"Write what down?"

"'You can't all be Paul.' And whatever else comes thereafter from your lips."

"No," said Kline, a strange dread starting to grow in him. "I don't want you to write anything down."

"Is that too a teaching?" said Paul. "'Write nothing down'?"

A *strange dread* is right—the Pauls have decided he is the Messiah, and they intend to give him the honor of a crucifixion. The other side is just as horrifying, the only difference in their plans for Kline being that they wish to crucify him as Barabbas, not Jesus. In two regards he does seem perhaps to be singled out by a larger force: Kline could be seen as harrowing an all-but literal hell as he goes about his murderous business, and no matter how great the odds against him, it comes to seem that he cannot be killed. So as he sinks deeper and deeper into a river of blood, in the process completely aware that he is losing, then has lost, his soul, Kline may either actually have become a holy figure, the new Messiah who brings not life but the gruesome Last Days and End Times, or he may be completely deluded, off his rocker, a nut case whack job. Evenson, thankfully, lets the ambiguity stand.

Instead of resolving Kline's worldly status, he does something far
more interesting. Reeking (one imagines) of smoke, covered in blood,
Kline listens to the sound of the approaching sirens and, having
nothing else to do, walks off. Soon he begins to jog, then settles into
straightforward running, asking himself *Where now?* and *What next?*
The last protagonist of a great work of American fiction to ask himself
these questions so resonantly was probably Huckleberry Finn.

In the afterword written for the 2002 University of Nebraska Press
republication of *Altmann's Tongue*, Evenson describes what befell him
when the Church of Jesus Christ of Latter-Day Saints, the institution
in which he was raised to be a faithful and believing Mormon, decided
to pose itself against his work, which it saw to be indulgent toward
violence and depraved in its outlook. (It seems that none of this was
made very explicit. The Church retreated into a prolix bureaucratic
boondoggle intended to wear him down and ended by requesting that
he prove his good faith by ceasing to write. The man was mugged by
his own religion.) It is difficult not to frame the sects in *Last Days* as
bleakly parodic versions of Mormonism, but to do so would be more
than a little reductive. Sure, Mormonism is in there, but so is a great
deal else.

Early on in his afterword, Evenson speaks of a period when he was
living in Seattle, studying and writing. He had agreed to serve as a
bishopric counselor and was sometimes asked to perform the tasks
of a transient bishop. In this role, he picked up stranded, homeless,
sometimes derelict people at certain specified locations and simply
drove them around the city, hearing them out and trying to figure out
how best to help them. Listening to what they had to say was central
to his mission as he defined it. At least once, he felt that the man beside
him represented serious danger.

The conclusion to his afterward pushes this situation up several
notches:

> "You have been driving in the car, a man pointing a gun
> at your head, and now he has left the car and you are free.
> Everything around you has gone strange. You are no longer in
> the same world you were in before the gun bruised your temple.
> You have the suspicion that you are no longer yourself.

"Now, now that you are free (if it really is you), the question
is, How do you make sense of the rest of your life?"

What are you doing, where are you going, who are you? After great extremity, everything in your life should be seen anew. The objects are pretty much the same, except of course that they contain within them the seeds of what happened to you, but the maps around and to them have all been redrawn. You can get lost in a second. Who you are is a puzzle it may take the rest of your life to solve, and in the end it may turn out that you are merely the person who spent his life trying to work out the puzzle of who he was. But that . . . that's not nothing.

THE BROTHERHOOD
OF MUTILATION

And if thy right eye offend thee, pluck it
out, and cast it from thee . . . And if thy
right hand offend thee, cut if off, and
cast it from thee . . .

Matthew 5:29–30

I.

It was only later that he realized the reason they had called him, but by then it was too late for the information to do him any good. At the time, all the two men had told him on the telephone was that they'd seen his picture in the paper, read about his infiltration and so-called heroism and how, even when faced with the man with the cleaver—or the "gentleman with the cleaver" as they chose to call him—he hadn't flinched, hadn't given a thing away. Was it true, they wanted to know, that he hadn't flinched? That he had simply watched the man raise the cleaver and bring it down, his hand suddenly becoming a separate, moribund creature?

He didn't bother to answer. He only sat holding the telephone receiver against his face with his remaining hand and looking at the stump that marked the end of the other arm. The shiny, slightly puckered termination of flesh, flaked and angry at its extreme.

"Who is this?" he finally asked.

The men on the other end of the telephone laughed. "This is opportunity knocking," one of them said, the one with the deeper voice. "Do you want to be trapped behind a desk the rest of your life, Mr. Kline?"

The other voice, the one with a lisp, kept asking questions. Was it true, it wanted to know, that after he had removed his belt with his remaining hand and tightened it as a tourniquet around the stump, he then stood up, turned on one of the burners on the stovetop, and cauterized the wound himself?

"Maybe," Kline said.

"Maybe to what?" asked Low Voice.

"I have it on authority that you did," said Lisp. "Was it electric or gas? I would think electric would be better. But then again it would take awhile for electric to warm up."

"It was a hotplate," said Kline.

"A hotplate?" said Low Voice. "Good Lord, a hotplate?"

"So, electric?" asked Lisp.

"I didn't have anything else," said Kline. "There was only a hotplate."

"And then, once cauterized, you turned around and shot him through the eye," said Lisp. "Left-handed no less."

"Maybe," said Kline. "But that wasn't in the papers. Who told you that?"

"I have it on authority," said Lisp. "That's all."

"Look," said Kline. "What's this all about?"

"Opportunity, Mr. Kline," said Low Voice. "I told you already."

"There's a plane ticket waiting under your name at the airport."

"Why?" asked Kline.

"Why?" asked Lisp. "Because we admire you, Mr. Kline."

"And we'd like your help."

"What sort of help?"

"We must have *you*, Mr. Kline. Nobody else will do," said Low Voice.

"No?" said Kline. "Why should I trust you? And who are you exactly?"

Lisp laughed.

"Mr. Kline," Lisp said, "surely by now you realize that you can't trust anyone. But why not take a chance?"

There was no reason to go. It was not a question, as Low Voice had suggested, of either a desk job or their offer, whatever their offer happened to be. The pension he had received was enough to live on. Plus, right after he had lost his hand and cauterized the wound himself and then shot the so-called gentleman with the cleaver through the eye, he had taken the liberty, in recompense for the loss of his hand, of helping himself to a briefcase containing several hundred thousand dollars. This he saw as a profoundly moral act in a kind of moral, biblical, old testament sense: an eye for a hand, and a bag of money thrown in. The fact that the eye had had a brain and a skull behind it was incidental.

So, in short, there was no reason to accept the invitation. Better to stay put, have a lifelike prosthetic made to fit over the stump or, at the very least, wear and learn how to use the hooks that had been given him. Perfect a game of one-handed golf. Purchase a drawerful of prosthetics for all occasions. Buy some cigars. All of life was open to him, he told himself. Opportunity could knock all it liked.

And besides, he was having trouble getting out of bed. Not that he was depressed, but it was hard to get out of bed especially when he remembered that the first thing he'd be doing was trying to brush his teeth left-handed. So, instead, he spent more and more time rubbing the end of his stump, or simply staring at it. It seemed, the termination of it, at once a part of him and not at all part of him, fascinating. Sometimes he still reached for things with his missing hand. Most days he couldn't even put on the hooks. And if he couldn't bring himself to strap on the hooks, how could he be expected to leave the house? And if he didn't leave the house, how could he be expected to go to the airport, let alone pick up the ticket, let alone board a plane?

Things will get better, he told his stump. *Someday we'll leave the house. Things are bound to improve.*

A week after the first call, they called back.

"You missed it," said Lisp. "You missed the flight."

"Is it because of fear?" asked Low Voice. "Are you afraid of flying?"

"How can you say that to him?" Lisp asked Low Voice. "A man who cauterizes his own stump isn't going to let a little something like that get to him, is he?"

"So he missed the flight," said Low Voice. "He didn't allow for enough time. Got held up at security, maybe."

"Yes," said Lisp. "That's sure to be it."

They both fell silent. Kline kept the receiver pressed against his ear.

"Well?" asked Lisp.

"Well what?" asked Kline.

"What happened?" asked Lisp.

"I didn't go."

"He didn't go," said Low Voice.

"We know that," said Lisp. "We know you didn't go, otherwise you'd be here. If you'd gone we wouldn't be calling you there."

"No," said Kline.

The phone was silent again. Kline listened to it, staring at the veiled window.

"So?" said Low Voice.

"So what?"

"Goddammit," said Lisp. "Do we have to go through this again?"

"Look," said Kline. "I don't even know who you are."

"We already told you who we are," said Lisp.

"We're opportunity," said Low Voice. "And we're knocking."

"I'm going to hang up," said Kline.

"He's hanging up," said Low Voice, his voice sounded worn out and exhausted.

"Wait!" said Lisp. "No!"

"Nothing personal," said Kline. "I'm just not your man."

Almost as soon as he hung up, the telephone began ringing again. He let it ring. He stood up and walked around the apartment, from room to room. There were four rooms, if you counted the bathroom as a room. In every one he could hear the telephone clearly. It kept ringing.

In the end, he picked up the receiver. "What?" he said.

"But you *are* our man," said Lisp, his voice desperate. "We're just like you."

"There's the ticket—" said Low Voice.

"No ticket," said Kline. "No opportunity. I'm not your man."

"Do you think we are acquaintances of the man with the hatchet?" asked Lisp.

"Cleaver," said Low Voice.

"We are not acquaintances of the man with the hatchet," Lisp said. "We're just like you."

"And what am I like, exactly?" said Kline.

"Come and see," said Low Voice. "Why not come and see?"

"If we wanted to kill you," Lisp said. "You'd be dead by now." It was odd, thought Kline, to be threatened by a man with a lisp.

"Please, Mr. Kline," said Low Voice.

"We don't want to kill you," said Lisp. "Ergo, you're still alive."

"Aren't you even a little curious, Mr. Kline?" asked Low Voice.

"No," said Kline. And hung up the telephone.

When the telephone began to ring again, he unplugged it from the wall. Rolling the cord up around it, he packed it away in the closet.

He walked around the house. He would have to go out, he realized, in a day or two, to buy food. He went into the bedroom and took, from the table beside the bed, a notepad and a pen. Going into the kitchen he opened all the doors of the cabinets, the refrigerator, the freezer, and sat thinking.

Eggs, he thought.

Eggs, he wrote, though doing it with his left hand it came out looking like *Esgs*.

My left hand doesn't want eggs, he thought. It wants *esgs*.

He kept writing, his left hand mutilating each word slightly. *What do you think of that?* he asked his stump. And then wondered if he was speaking to his stump or to his missing hand. Did it matter? he wondered. He wondered what had become of his hand. Probably it had stayed on the table where it had been cut off. Probably it had still been there when the police arrived and had been taken away to be frozen and marked as an exhibit. It was probably still frozen somewhere.

Esgs it is, he thought. And *dread*. And maybe a glass or two of *nelk*.

He stared at the notepad, stopped staring only when he heard water dripping out of the defrosting freezer. He was not sure how much time had passed.

He got up and closed the freezer and fridge, and then stood waiting, listening for the motor to kick in.

◆◆◆

A few days went by. His electric razor broke, emitting only a low hum when he plugged it in. He stopped shaving. The food mostly ran out. *I need to get some food*, he thought, but instead drank a glass of sour milk.

He lay in the bed, holding the milk-ghosted glass with one hand, balanced on his chest. He could get up, he thought. He could get out of bed and get up and get out of the house. *I need to get some food*, he thought, and then thought, *later*. There would always be time to get food later. *Esgs* and *dread*. At some point he realized that the glass he had thought he was holding was being held with his missing hand. The glass was balanced on his chest, the stump stationed beside it, a blunt animal. He was not quite sure how the glass had got there.

He was not going out, he realized hours later. The milk still ringing the bottom of the glass had dried into a white sheet and had begun to crack. Perhaps it was days later. He had missed his chance, he realized, and now what little will he had had slipped away and it was too late. He closed his eyes. When he opened them it was dark outside, so he closed them again.

When he opened them, a pale daylight leaked into the room through the curtains. Beside him, sitting on kitchen chairs they had dragged into the bedroom, were two men. They were bundled in heavy coats and gloves and scarves despite the warmth of the room.

"Hello, hello," said the first, his voice bass.

"We knocked," said the other. His upper lip was mostly missing, a ragged scar in its place; it looked as if the lip had been cut into with a pair of pinking shears. "We knocked and knocked, but nobody answered. So we let ourselves in. It was locked," he said, "but we knew you didn't mean the lock for us."

When Kline didn't say anything, the one with the torn lip said, "You remember us? The telephone?" The man lisped on the *us*, but having seen the lip it was hard for him to think of him as just Lisp anymore.

"The telephone," said Kline, his voice raspy.

The torn-lipped man raised his eyebrows and looked at his companion. "He's pretending not to remember," he said.

"Of course you remember," said the one with the bass voice. "Opportunity knocking? All that?"

"Ah," said Kline. "I'm afraid so."

"Look at you," said Torn-Lip. "Do you want to die in bed?"

"You don't want to die in bed," said Low Voice.

"We're here to save you," said Torn-Lip.

"I don't want to be saved," said Kline.

"He doesn't want to be saved," said Low Voice.

"Sure he does," said Torn-Lip. "He just doesn't know it yet."

"But I—"

"Mr. Kline," said Torn-Lip, "we have given you every opportunity to be reasonable. Why didn't you take advantage of either of the tickets we left for you?"

"I don't need your ticket," said Kline.

"When was the last time you ate?" asked Low Voice.

Torn-Lip reached out and prodded Kline's face with a gloved finger. "Clearly, you are your own worst enemy, Mr. Kline."

"Depression," said Low Voice. "Lassitude, ennui. I so diagnose."

"Look," said Kline, struggling to lift himself up a little in the bed. "I'm going to have to ask you to leave."

"He sits," said Torn-Lip.

"Or nearly so. Who says the man doesn't have any fight left to him?"

"That's the spirit," said Torn-Lip. "That's the man who can have his hand cut off and not flinch."

"Come away with us, Mr. Kline."

"No," said Kline.

"What can we say to convince you?"

"Nothing," said Kline.

"Well, then," said Torn-Lip. "Perhaps there are means other than words."

Kline watched as the man grasped one of his gloved hands with the other. He twisted the hand about and levered it downward and the hand came free. Kline felt his stump tingle. The other man, he saw, was doing the same thing. They pulled back their sleeves to show him the bare exposed lumps of flesh in which their forearms terminated.

"You see," said Torn-Lip, "just like you."

"Come with us," said the other.

"But," said Kline. "I don't—"

"He thinks we're asking," said Torn-Lip, leaning in over the bed, his damaged mouth livid. "We're not asking. We're telling."

II.

Before he knew it, their hands were screwed back on and they had him
out of the bed and were dragging him down the emergency stairwell.

"Wait," he said. "My claw."

"Your claw?"

"For my hand."

You don't need it, they claimed, and kept pulling him down the stairs.

"Where are you taking me?" he asked.

"He wants to know where we're taking him, Ramse," said Low Voice.

"To the car," said Torn-Lip—said Ramse—grunting the words. They
came to a landing and Kline felt his own body sway to one side and
then steady itself. Ramse was beside him, his head sticking out from
under Kline's arm, his lips, torn and whole, tight against each other.
"Tell him we're going to the car," Ramse said.

"We're going to the car," said Low Voice, and Kline looked over to
find Low Voice's head under the other arm.

"But," he said.

"Enough questions," said Ramse. "Just try to move your feet. If you
have them, may as well use them."

He looked down and could not see feet, only legs. There was a
whispery sound, but it wasn't until they left the landing and started
down the next set of stairs and the sound changed to a thumping that
he realized it was his own feet dragging. He tried to get his feet
underneath him, but the two men were moving too quickly and all he
could do was to nearly trip them all down the stairs.

"Never mind, never mind," said Ramse. "We're almost there." And indeed, Kline realized, they were pushing through the fire exit door and into full sunlight. There was a car there, long and black with tinted windows. They hustled him into the back of it.

Ramse got in on the driver's side, Low Voice on the other. There was something wrong with the steering wheel, Kline noticed, as if a cup holder had been welded into it. Low Voice opened the glove box, awkwardly groped a candy bar out of it with his artificial hand, passed it back to Kline.

"Eat this," he said. "It'll help focus you."

Kline heard the locks snap down. He took the candy bar, began to strip the wrapper off it. It was almost more than he could manage. In the front, the two men were shucking their coats and hats, piling them on the seat between them. He watched Ramse snap off his artificial hand, glove and all, and drop it atop the pile. Low Voice did the same.

"That's better," Low Voice said.

Kline ate a little of the candy bar. It was chocolate, something crispy inside it. He chewed. Ramse, he realized, was holding his remaining hand up, toward the other man.

"Gous?" Ramse asked.

"What?" the man said. "Yes, right," Gous said. "Sorry."

With his single hand he reached out and took Ramse's remaining hand and twisted it. Kline watched the hand circle about and break free. Ramse rubbed his two stumps against each other. Gous reached out and took hold of Ramse's ear, tore it off. It came free, leaving a gaping unwhelked hole behind.

"There," said Ramse. "That's better." He looked at Kline in the rearview mirror, lifted up both stumps. "Like you," he said, smiling. "Only more so."

They drove, the city slowly dissolving around them and breaking up into fields and trees. Gous kept rummaging in the glove box, passing back food. There was another candy bar, a plastic bag of broken pretzels, a tin of sardines. Kline took a little of each, left what remained on the seat beside him. He was beginning to feel a little more alert. Outside, the sun was high; even through the tinted glass it looked hot outside. They turned right and went up a ramp and entered the freeway, the car quickly gaining speed.

"Where are we?" Kline asked.

"Here we go," said Gous, ignoring him.

"Smooth sailing from here on out," said Ramse. "For a while anyway."

"But," said Kline. "Where, I don't—"

"Mr. Kline," said Gous. "Please sit back and enjoy the ride."

"What else?" asked Kline.

"What else?" said Gous.

"What do you mean what else?" asked Ramse.

"What else comes off."

"Besides the hands and the ear?" said Ramse. "Some toes," he said, "but they're already off. Three gone from one foot, two from the other."

"What happened?" asked Kline.

"What do you mean *what happened*, Mr. Kline? Nothing *happened*."

"We don't do accidents," said Gous. "Accidents and acts of God don't mean a thing, unless they're followed later by acts of will. Pretzel?" he asked.

"Your own case was hotly debated," said Ramse. "Some wanted to classify it as an accident."

"But it was no accident," said Gous.

"No," said Ramse. "Others argued, successfully, that it was no accident but instead an act of will. But then the question came 'An act of will on whose part?' On the part of the gentleman with the hatchet, surely, no denying that, but responsibility can hardly rest solely with him, can it now, Mr. Kline?" He turned a little around as he said it, pivoting his missing ear toward Kline. "All you had to do was tell him one thing, Mr. Kline, just a lie, and you would have kept your hand. But you didn't say a thing. A matter of will, Mr. Kline. Your will to lose the hand far outweighed your will to retain it."

Outside, the highway had narrowed to a two-lane road, cutting through dry scraggled woods, the road's shoulder heaped in dust.

"What about you?" Kline asked Gous.

"Me?" said Gous, blushing. "Just the hand," he said. "I'm still new."

"Have to start somewhere," said Ramse. "We brought him along because the powers that be thought you might be more comfortable with someone like you."

"He's not like me."

"You have one amputation, he has one amputation," said Ramse. "Yours is a hand, his is a hand. In that sense, he's like you. When you start to look closer, well . . ."

"I used anesthetic," said Gous.

"You, Mr. Kline, did not use anesthetic. You weren't given that option."

"It's frowned upon," said Gous, "but not forbidden."

"And more or less expected for the first several amputations," said Ramse. "This makes you exceptional, Mr. Kline."

Kline looked at the seat next to him, the open tin of sardines, the filets shining in their oil.

"I'm exceptional as well," said Ramse. "I've never been anesthetized."

"He's an inspiration to us all," said Gous.

"But that you cauterized your wound yourself, Mr. Kline," said Ramse. "That makes you truly exceptional."

"I'd like to get out of the car now," said Kline softly.

"Don't be ridiculous, Mr. Kline," said Gous, grinning. "We're in the middle of nowhere."

"I could count the number of people who self-cauterize on one finger of one hand," said Ramse.

"If he had a hand," said Gous.

"If I had a hand," said Ramse.

They drove for a while in silence. Kline stayed as still as he could in the back seat. The sun had slid some little way down the horizon. After a while it vanished. The tin of sardines had slid down the seat and was now at an angle, the oil leaking slowly out. He straightened the tin, then rubbed his fingers dry on the floor carpeting. It was hard not to stare at Ramse's missing ear. He looked down at his own stump, looked at Gous' stump balanced on the seat's back. The two stumps were actually quite different, he thought. The end of Gous' was puckered. His own had been puckered and scarred from the makeshift cauterization; after the fact, a doctor had cut a little higher and smoothed it off, planed it.

Outside, the trees, already sparse, seemed to vanish almost entirely, perhaps partly because of the gathering darkness but also the landscape was changing. Ramse pushed one of his stumps into the panel and turned on the headlights.

"Eight," said Ramse, gesturing his head slightly backward.

"Eight?" asked Kline. "Eight what?"

"Amputations," said Ramse. Kline watched the back of his head. "Of course that doesn't mean a thing," he said. "Could be just eight toes, all done under anesthetic, the big toes left for balance. That should hardly qualify for an eight," he said.

Gous nodded next to him. He held up his stump, looked over the back. "This counts as a one," he said. "But I could have left the hand and cut off all the fingers and I'd be a four. Five if you took the thumb."

They were waiting for Kline to say something. "That hardly seems fair," he offered.

"But which is more of a shock?" asked Ramse. "A man losing his fingers or a man losing his hand?"

Kline didn't know if he was expected to answer. "I'd like to get out of the car," he said.

"So there are eights," said Ramse, "and then there are eights." They came to a curve. Kline watched Ramse post the other hand on the steering wheel for balance, turning the wheel with his cupped stump. "Personally I prefer a system of minor and major amputations, according to which I'd be a 2/3."

"I prefer by weight," said Gous. "Weigh the lopped-off member, I say."

"But you see," said Ramse, "bled or unbled? And doesn't that give a certain advantage to the corpulent?"

"You develop standards," said Gous. "Penalties and handicaps."

"Why do you need me?" asked Kline.

"Excuse me?" asked Ramse.

"He wants to know why we need him," said Gous.

"That's easy," said Ramse. "A crime has been committed."

"Why me?" asked Kline.

"You have a certain amount of experience in investigation," said Gous.

"Not investigation exactly, but infiltration," said Ramse.

"And you don't flinch, Mr. Kline," said Gous.

"No, he doesn't flinch."

"But—" said Kline.

"You'll be briefed," said Ramse. "You'll be told what to do."

"But the police—"

"No police," said Ramse. "It was hard enough to get the others to agree on you."

"If it hadn't been for the hand," said Gous.

"If it hadn't been for the hand," said Ramse, "you wouldn't be here. But you're one of us, like it or not."

III.

He woke up when the car stopped in front of a set of metal gates. It was fully dark outside.

"Almost there," said Ramse from the front.

The gates opened a little and a small man stepped out, turning pale and white in the over-bright halogen glow of the headlights. The man came over to the driver's door. Kline could see he was missing an eye, one closed lid seeming flat and deflated. He was wearing a uniform. Ramse rolled down the window, and the man peered into the car.

"Mr. Ramse," said the guard. "And Mr. Gous. Who's in the back?"

"That would be Mr. Kline," said Ramse. "Hold up your arm, Mr. Kline," said Ramse.

Kline lifted his hand.

"No, the other one," said Ramse.

He lifted the stumped arm and the guard nodded. "A one?" he asked.

"Right," said Ramse. "But self-cauterized."

The guard whistled. He drew away from the window and made his way back to the gates, which he drew open just wide enough for the car to pass through. Through the rear window, Kline watched him draw the gates shut after them.

"Welcome home, Mr. Kline," said Ramse.

Kline didn't say anything.

They passed a row of houses, turned down a smaller road where the houses were a little more spread out, then down a third, smaller, tree-lined alley that dead-ended in front of a small, two-story building. Ramse stopped the car. The three of them climbed out.

"You'll be staying here, Mr. Kline," said Ramse. "First floor, second door to the left once you go through the entrance. There's probably an hour or two of night left," he said. "We'll see you in the morning. For now, why don't you try to get some sleep?"

When he went in, he couldn't figure out how to turn the hall light on so, instead, wandered down the dark hall dragging his hand along the wall, feeling for doorways. His fingers stuttered past one. He lifted his fingers from the wall and brought them near his face. They smelled of dust. He went on until he came to another doorframe, fumbled around for the handle.

Inside, he found a switch. It was a small windowless room, containing a narrow single bed with a thin, ratty blanket. In one corner was a metal cabinet. The floor was linoleum, a streaked blue. The light, he saw, was a naked bulb, hanging from the center of the ceiling. The walls' paint was cracking.

Welcome home, he thought.

He closed the door. There was no lock on it. He opened the cabinet. It was full of stacks of calendars, each month featuring a woman in various states of undress, smiling furiously. He looked at the first picture for some time before realizing the girl was missing one of her thumbs. With each month, the losses became more obvious and more numerous, March losing a breast, July missing both breasts, a hand, and a forearm. The December girl was little more than a torso, her breasts shaved off, wearing nothing but a thin white cloth banner from one shoulder to the opposite hip, reading "Miss Less Is More."

He put the calendar back and closed the cabinet. Turning off the light he lay in the bed, but kept seeing Miss Less Is More's face contorted with joy. There was Ramse's face too, his mutilated ear just above the car seatback angling itself toward him. His own stump was tingling. He got up and turned on the light, tried to sleep with it on.

He dreamt that he was sitting at the table again, the gentleman with the cleaver standing before him, cleaver coming down. Only in his dream he wasn't just the man losing his hand but also the man with the cleaver. He watched himself bring the cleaver down and the hand come free and the fingers pulse. The sheared plane of his wrist grew pale and then suddenly puffed, blood pulsing out. He stripped off his belt with his remaining hand and tightened it quickly around his arm until the bleeding slowed and mostly stopped. He watched himself do it, holding the cleaver in his hand. Then he watched himself, pale and holding the belt tight, go to the stove and turn it on, wait for the coils of the burner to smoke and begin to glow. He pushed his stump down and heard it sizzle and smelt the burnt flesh, and when he lifted the stump away it was smoking. Bits of flesh and blood were stuck to the burner and smoldering.

Then, with his left hand, face livid with pain, he took out his gun and, left-handed, shot himself through the eye. It was a hell of a thing to watch, a hell of a thing to feel. And as soon as it was over it started again, and kept starting until he forced himself awake.

Gous and Ramse were in the room, the first standing at the open cabinet looking through the calendar, rubbing at his crotch with his stump, the second standing near the bed, looking at Kline.

"Rise and shine," said Ramse.

Kline sat on the edge of the bed, pulling his pants on awkwardly with stump and arm. Ramse watched. Only when he was done did he say, "There's new clothes for you."

"Where?" asked Kline.

"Gous has them," said Ramse. "Gous?" he said, louder.

"What?" said Gous, turning stiffly away from the calendar, face red with shame or heat, or perhaps both.

"Clothes, Gous," said Ramse.

"Oh, right," said Gous, and picking up a pile of clothing near his feet, threw it to Kline.

As Ramse watched, Kline stripped out of the clothes he had just put on. The new clothing consisted of a pair of gray slacks, a white shirt, a red clip-on tie. The buttons weren't easy one-handed, particularly since the shirt was freshly starched, but after the first three they got easier. He tried to leave the tie on the bed, but Ramse stopped him.

"Put it on," he said.

"Why?"

"I'm wearing one, Gous is wearing one," said Ramse. And indeed, Kline had failed to notice, their outfits were the same as his: white shirts, gray slacks, red clip-on tie. He found himself wondering how Ramse had managed to put on his shirt by himself. Perhaps he hadn't.

"Let's go," said Gous once Kline's tie was on, and nudged him toward the exit.

"Look," said Ramse, as they went out the door and started to walk down the drive. "Things are done in a certain way here. We hope you'll try to respect that."

"All right," said Kline.

"The other thing," said Ramse. "The investigation."

"He's taking you to Borchert," said Gous.

"I'm taking you to Borchert," said Ramse. 'He'll tell you about the investigation."

"Who's Borchert?"

"It's not who's Borchert," said Ramse, "but what he is. And what he is is a twelve."

"A twelve?"

"That's right," said Gous, then rattled off in a schoolboy's voice, "Leg, toe, toe, toe, toe, toe, left arm, finger, finger, ear, eye, ear."

"A twelve," said Ramse. "Of course that includes a lot of digits, but when you add in two lopped limbs, it's impressive."

"He's second in command," said Gous. "After Aline."

"I see," said Kline. "What's the investigation about?"

"We don't know," said Gous.

"Borchert will tell you," said Ramse.

"You don't know?" asked Kline.

"I know a little. I should know more," said Ramse wistfully. "I'm an eight. There's no reason to keep me in the dark. Gous is another story."

"I'm just a one," admitted Gous.

"He's just a one," said Ramse, smiling. "At least for now."

"I'm a one too," said Kline.

"That's right," said Gous to Ramse. "He's a one but he's going to find out."

"He's an exception," said Ramse. "He's the exception that proves the rule."

"Why?" asked Kline. They came to a small path cutting away from the road, paved with crushed white shells. Ramse and Gous stepped onto it, Kline followed.

"Yes, why?" asked Gous.

"How the hell should I know," asked Ramse. "I'm an eight. They don't always tell me everything. Maybe because he's a self-cauterizer."

"Listen," said Kline. "I'll see Borchert and talk to him, but that's it. I'm not interested in staying."

"Borchert can be very persuasive," said Ramse.

"Don't insult Borchert," said Gous. "Be polite to him, listen to him, don't talk back."

"He's a twelve," said Ramse. "Plus his leg's amputated at the hip. That's commitment for you, eh?".

"He stayed awake for the operation," said Gous.

"But he had anesthetic," said Ramse.

"Still," said Gous.

"What about cauterization?" asked Kline.

"The cauterization?" asked Gous. "Don't know. Ramse, was he anesthetized for that too?"

"Don't know," said Ramse. "Probably. In any case, he didn't self-cauterize."

"Almost nobody does," said Gous.

"Really nobody but you," said Ramse.

The path moved back into trees, descending into a sort of depression. Kline saw, affixed to an old oak, a security camera. Then the path took a sharp curve and started uphill again. It widened into a tree-lined avenue, at the end of which was what looked like an old manor house, or a boarding school, made of gray stone. Kline counted six sets of windows in rows three tall.

They reached the gate, Kline listening to the shells crunching beneath his feet. A guard came out from behind a pillar of the house and stood on the opposite side of the gate, watching them with a single eye.

"What is wanted?" he asked, his hands folded.

"Cut it out," said Ramse. "This isn't ceremonial. We're here to see Borchert."

"Borchert?" said the guard. "What is wanted?"

"Cut it out," said Ramse. "This is Kline."

"Kline?" said the guard, unfolding his arms to reveal hands shorn of all but a thumb, a forefinger, and a middle finger. He took hold of the key and fitted it to the lock. "Why didn't you say so?" the guard said. "Let him enter."

"Are all the guards missing an eye?" asked Kline.

"Yes," Gous said happily. "All of them."

"They made a pact," said Ramse, knocking on the door. "It's a subsect. Whatever else they're missing they cut out the eye once they're initiated. Borchert started down that path," said Ramse. "He was a guard initiate, and then gave it up. What his connection to the guards is now isn't quite clear, is mysterious. That's why he's second in command, not first."

"And the eye's not all," said Gous.

"No?" said Kline.

"Let's just say that a guard can hit all the high notes and none of the low ones."

"Well," said Ramse, "nobody knows about that for certain except the guards. And they don't discuss it."

The door was opened by another guard who asked again, "What is wanted?" This time Ramse brought his heels together and rattled off what to Kline seemed clearly a memorized, ritual response. "Having been faithful in all things, we come to see he who is even more faithful than we."

"That is correct," said the guard. "And what are the three of you?"

"Two ones," said Gous. "And an eight."

"Which is the eight?"

"I am," said Ramse.

"You may enter," said the guard. "The others may not."

"But we're here with Kline," said Ramse. "We're bringing Kline to Borchert."

"Kline?" said the guard. "We've been waiting for him. He can come in, too, the other one will have to wait outside."

Kline felt something on his shoulder and looked back to see Gous' stump lying there. "A pleasure, Mr. Kline," Gous said. "Don't forget me."

"I won't," said Kline, confused.

The guard ushered them through the gate and into a bare, white hall. Before the door closed Kline looked behind him to see Gous on the other side, tilting his head trying to see in.

This guard, Kline saw, had only one hand, all the fingers on it shaved away except for the thumb and the bottom half of the forefinger.

The guard led them down the white hall to a door at the end, knocked three times.

"You're lucky," said Ramse.

"Lucky?"

"To come in," said Ramse. "Normally a one wouldn't be allowed. There had to be a special dispensation."

"I don't feel lucky," said Kline. The guard turned around and looked at him, hard, then turned away, rapped three more times.

"Don't say that," whispered Ramse. "You don't know how hard it was to convince them to bring you."

The door came open, another guard pushing his face out. Ramse and Kline watched their guard push his face in and whisper to the other. They whispered back and forth a few times then the other guard nodded, opened the door.

"Go ahead," said the first guard. "Go through."

Ramse and Kline passed through the door, the second guard letting them come in and then shutting it behind them. Inside was a stairwell. The guard led them up it to the third floor, led them down a hall, past three doors, stopped to knock on a fourth. When a muffled voice answered from behind, he opened it, ushered them in.

The room was large, Spartan in furnishing: a bed sitting low to the floor, a low desk, a small bookshelf, a reclining chair. In the latter sat a man wearing a bathrobe. He was missing an arm and a leg, his robe cut away and left open at shoulder and hip to reveal the planed surfaces, hardly stumps at all. The other arm and leg were intact, though the hand was missing all but two of its fingers, the foot all but the big toe. Both ears, too, had been cut off, leaving only a hole and a shiny patch of flesh on either side of the head. One eyelid was open, revealing a piercing eye, the other closed but deflated, the eye under it clearly absent.

"Ah," said the man. "Mr. Kline, I presume. I had assumed you had refused our invitation several weeks ago."

"It seems not," said Kline.

"He's delighted to be here," said Ramse, quickly. "It's a true pleasure for him, as well as for me, sir, to be granted audience with—"

"I wonder," said Borchert, raising his voice. "Mr. Ramse, isn't it?"

"Yes," said Ramse, "I'm—"

"I wonder, Mr. Ramse, if you'd mind waiting outside. Mr. Kline and I have private matters to discuss."

"Oh," said Ramse, looking crestfallen. "Yes, of course."

"An eight," said Borchert, once Ramse was gone, "though you wouldn't know it to look at him. What does he mean by wearing shoes in here? Where are his manners?"

"Do you want me to take my shoes off?"

"Are you missing any toes?"

"No," said Kline.

"There's no point then, is there?" said Borchert. "But come a little closer and show me your stump."

Kline went closer. He held his missing hand out; Borchert took it deftly between his remaining fingers and thumb and pulled it forward until it was only inches from his face, his eyes dilating.

"Yes, nicely done," said Borchert. "Quite professional. But I'd thought you were a self-cauterizer?"

"I was," said Kline. "It was redone afterwards."

"What a shame," said Borchert, smiling thinly. "Still, a good start nonetheless." He let go of Kline's hand, readjusted himself in his chair. "You're welcome to sit down," he said. "Unfortunately I'm in the only chair. Do feel free to help yourself to the floor."

Kline looked about him, finally settling to the floor, posting his stump against it and bringing the rest of his body down.

"There," said Borchert. "That's better now, isn't it. I suppose you're wondering why you're here."

"The investigation," said Kline.

"The investigation," said Borchert. "That's right. You want the details."

"No," said Kline.

"No?"

"I'm wondering how I can arrange to leave."

"Leave me?" said Borchert. "You find me offensive somehow?"

"Leave this whole place."

"But why, Mr. Kline?" said Borchert, smiling. "This is paradise."

Kline did not say anything.

Borchert let his smile fade slowly, artificially. "I was against bringing you," he said. "I don't mind telling you. *No outsiders* has always been my policy, and no recruiting. But some of the others were impressed by this story of self-cauterization. Perhaps it's nothing more than a story, Mr. Kline?"

"No," said Kline. "It's true."

"But why, Mr. Kline? Surely you could have easily applied a tourniquet and called a doctor?"

"Then I wouldn't have been able to kill the man who cut my hand off."

"The so-called gentleman with the cleaver," said Borchert, nodding. "But surely you could have killed the fellow later?"

"No," said Kline. "It was either him or me, right then. I cauterized the arm to distract him. He couldn't quite take in what I was doing, which gave me a certain advantage. Otherwise, he would have shot me."

"Yet you could take it in, Mr. Kline, even though it was your own arm. And afterwards your remaining hand was steady enough to shoot him through the eye. You were God for a moment, even if you didn't realize it. I suspect you tapped into something without knowing it, Mr. Kline. An ecstasy. I almost begin to suspect we have something to learn from you."

"I wouldn't think so," said Kline.

"Modest, too," said Borchert. "You know what you've done to our community? You've started something, Mr. Kline. Everybody is talking about self-cauterization. The creed is threatening to transform. Schism. No self-cauterizers yet, but it's only a matter of time, and then smoothly cut surfaces," he said, gesturing at his missing arm and leg, "are likely to give way to hard-puckered and rippled stumps, ugly and dappled. A little bit rough trade, no? I can't say it's to my taste, Mr. Kline, but perhaps I'm becoming antiquated."

"Perhaps," said Kline.

Borchert looked at him sharply. "I doubt it," he said. "In any case, Mr. Kline, despite my personal objections to you, now that you are here, I can't afford to let you go. Too much is at stake. I send you out of here without an investigation and we'll have a schism."

"I'm not staying," said Kline.

"You leave and I'll have to kill you," said Borchert. "For the good of the faith. Nothing personal."

Kline looked at his hand, then looked at Borchert.

"Wouldn't you like to at least hear about it, Mr. Kline? Before deciding if it's worth dying for?"

"All right," said Kline. "Why not?"

"A crime has been committed. You are not to discuss the specific details of this crime with anyone with fewer than ten amputations. Do I make myself clear?"

"Yes," said Kline.

"And in any case, Mr. Kline, I expect you to be discreet. This is a somewhat precarious society. The only one who knows the full extent of this crime is myself and, in a moment, yourself."

Kline just nodded.

"In short, we've had a murder," said Borchert.

"A murder," said Kline. "Murder's not exactly my specialty."

"No," said Borchert. "But you're all we have."

"May I ask who was murdered?"

"A man called Aline," said Borchert. "He organized this community, this brotherhood. A prophet, a visionary. Both arms lopped off at the shoulder, legs gone, penis severed, ears removed, eyes removed, tongue cut partly out, teeth removed, lips peeled away, nipples sliced off, buttocks gone. Anything that could be removed removed. A true visionary. Murdered."

"How was he murdered?"

"Someone broke open his sternum, chopped his heart out."

"Do you have any idea who—"

"No," said Borchert. "And we'd like the heart back if possible."

"Why do you need the heart back?"

Borchert smiled. "Mr. Kline," he said. "We're a brotherhood. This is a religion. His heart means something to us."

Kline shrugged.

"I don't expect you to understand," said Borchert. "You're an outsider. But perhaps you'll understand one day." He moved awkwardly in his chair. "By the way," he said, "What became of your own hand?"

"I don't know," said Kline.

"You don't know," said Borchert. "Imagine that. Colonel Pierre Souvestre's leg was buried in a full-blown state funeral when he lost it in 1917. Your hand, on the other hand, is probably rotting in a pile of garbage somewhere."

Kline stood up. "When can I see the body?" he asked.

Borchert sighed. "I've told you everything you need to know about it," he said. "There's no need to see the body."

"You don't have the body anymore?"

"No," said Borchert. "It's not that."

"Then what?"

"His body is sacred to us," said Borchert. "Even without the heart."

"Are there any witnesses?"

"You're not to approach anyone with more than ten amputations without an invitation."

Kline looked about the room. "That makes the investigation a little difficult."

"I'm sure you'll manage," Borchert said.

"Can I at least see the room?"

"Yes," said Borchert, slowly. "I suppose we could manage that."

"So I'm to investigate a murder without seeing a body and without being able to interview witnesses or suspects?"

"Don't exaggerate, Mr. Kline. Just don't break in on anyone unannounced. Talk to me and I'll make arrangements."

Turning, Kline made for the door.

"Oh, and one more thing, Mr. Kline," said Borchert.

"What's that?" asked Kline.

Borchert held up one of his two remaining fingers. "As an act of good faith," he said, "to show you I have nothing against self-cauterization, that I'm an open-minded man, I'd like your help removing the upper joint of this."

"You want me to cut it off."

"Just the top joint," Borchert said. "Little more than a symbolic gesture, a pact if you will. You'll find a cleaver in the top drawer," he said, gesturing to the back of the room with a flick of his head. "There's a stove there as well, Mr. Kline, built into the counter, which I'll ask you to turn on."

Kline looked at him, looked into the back of the room, shrugged.
"Why not?" he asked.

Opening the drawer, he removed the cleaver. He placed it on the
counter, resting it on a butcher's block, the wood of which was laced
with dozens of thin crosshatched marks. He went back to Borchert,
and dragged his chair to the back of the room, set it flush against
the counter.

"You don't know what an honor this is for you," said Borchert. "It's
quite a gesture of intimacy. Almost anyone here would kill for it. A
shame it's wasted on you."

"I'll take your word for it," said Kline.

He took Borchert by the wrist and placed the hand on the butcher's
block. He folded the index finger back into Borchert's palm, leaving
the remaining finger, the middle finger, angled down against the
butcher's block. The burner had warmed now and was glowing red,
smoking slightly. He rested his stump just above Borchert's knuckle
and held the finger steady, pushed it down slightly so that the first
joint was firmly against the wood.

"Just the first joint?" he asked.

Borchert smiled. "For now," he said.

He lifted the cleaver and brought it down hard and fast, as had been
done to him, to his hand. The blade was sharp; there was almost no
resistance as it went through the joint, perhaps a slight snap as it
chopped through bone. The finger's nail and the flesh and bone just
below it sat on one side of the blade, the rest of the finger on the other.
Borchert's face, he saw, had gone pale.

"Well done," said Borchert, his voice strained. "Now, Mr. Kline, if
you would see your way clear of releasing my hand . . ."

Looking down, Kline realized that his stump was pushing down on
Borchert's hand so hard that Borchert couldn't move. Blood was sputtering
a little out of the finger's end, weakly. He lifted his stump and Borchert
moved his finger away from the blade slightly and blood came puddling
up now against the blade. He watched Borchert swing the hand about
and, stretching his arm, bring the fingertip down onto the burner coil.

The flesh hissed, the blood hissing too, the air quickly filling with a smell that seemed to Kline like the smell of his own burning flesh. *Now*, he thought, *it is time for Borchert to pick up the gun and shoot me through the eye.* When Borchert took his finger away, Kline could still hear it hissing a little.

And then Borchert turned to face him, his face wreathed in ecstasy, his eyes dilated wide.

IV.

He was allowed to go back to his room and rest. He seemed to be the only one occupying the house, despite there being a half-dozen other rooms. Gous brought him a tray of food at lunchtime, and Gous sat at the small table with him while he ate, querying him gently about what Borchert had said. Kline didn't answer.

"Of course I understand," said Gous. "There's an order to these things. A one can't be told much."

"Where's Ramse?" asked Kline.

Gous shrugged. "Ramse was needed elsewhere," he said. "We're not glued at the hip."

Kline nodded, cutting into his meat—pork he thought—with his knife, keeping the plate from sliding with his stump. He put down the knife, picked up the fork, speared the meat.

"Do you know Aline?" he asked, once he had finished chewing.

"Aline?" asked Gous. "Everybody knows Aline. Not personally, maybe, but we know him. He's the prophet. He's the great one."

"Gous," said Kline. "Don't take this the wrong way, but how did you get involved in all this?"

"In all what?"

"All this," said Kline, gesturing with his stump. "This whole place." He reached out and took hold of Gous' stump. "In this," he said.

"Ramse," said Gous. "He got me started."

"He came up to you and said, 'Why don't you hack that off?'"

"It's not something I'm supposed to talk about," said Gous. "Not with outsiders."

"Am I an outsider, Gous?"

"Well," said Gous. "Yes and no."

"Here I am," said Kline. "I'm right here, just like you."

"True," said Gous.

"I've talked with Borchert," said Kline. "Have you talked with Borchert?"

"No," said Gous.

"Well, then?"

Gous held his head with his hand. "I'm not supposed to talk about it," he said.

"It's a secret," said Kline.

"Not secret, sacred," said Gous. He looked straight at Kline. "When you have the call, you'll know," he said.

"Maybe I've already had the call."

"Maybe," said Gous. "It's not for me to say."

He spent the day thinking. Aline was dead, the cult in crisis. What he was being called upon to do was to investigate, discover the murderer, and thus redeem the cult, allow it to go on. Was that right? Yet, according to Borchert he would not be allowed to see the body, would have to ask permission to interview anyone, would be monitored every step of the way. Was he really there to investigate at all, or was he simply Borchert's concession to someone else?

Near dark Ramse arrived, a basket full of food slung over one of his arms.

"Well, well," he said as he set the basket down on the table. "Had a good day?"

"Fair," said Kline. He opened the basket, dished up the food. There were two plates, so he gave some to Ramse as well.

"Borchert's quite a fellow, no?"

"Yes, quite."

"They don't make them better than that," said Ramse. "And a twelve too, to boot."

"Thirteen," said Kline. He began eating. Ramse, he noticed, wasn't touching his food.

"Thirteen?" asked Ramse, looking stricken. "What do you mean?"

"He had me cut off something."

"Leg, toe, toe, toe, toe, toe, left arm, finger, finger, ear, eye, ear. What else?"

"Finger," said Kline.

"The whole finger?"

"Just the first joint," said Kline.

"That hardly counts as a thirteen," said Ramse, looking relieved.

"You're not eating," said Kline.

"No," said Ramse.

"You already ate?"

"I don't have any hands," said Ramse. "You'll have to feed me when you're done."

Kline nodded, began to eat more quickly. When he was done, he pulled Ramse's plate closer, dipped his spoon in, lifted the spoon to Ramse's mouth. Ramse positioned his mouth so that the spoon's handle fit snugly into the lip's tear. It was hard for Kline not to stare at it.

"Do you have a picture of Aline?" he asked.

Ramse shook his head. "No pictures," he said. "The man's a prophet."

"That doesn't mean you can't have a picture."

"We're not Catholics," said Ramse between mouthfuls. "Or Mormons. Besides, we're concentrating on his absence, not his presence, on what he's severed rather than what remains."

Kline nodded. He kept shoveling food onto the spoon, lifting it into Ramse's mouth. *Not even the presence of an absence*, he thought, *but absence as absence proper. It shouldn't be called a twelve, but a minus twelve.*

"Ramse," said Kline, once the food was gone. "How did you get involved?"

"Involved," asked Ramse. "I'm an eight, aren't I? They can't withhold everything from me."

"Not in the investigation," said Kline. "In the cult."

Ramse stared at him. "First of all, it's not a cult," he said. "Second, I can't tell you."

"That's what Gous said."

Ramse smiled. "Why do you want to know?"

"I don't know," said Kline. "Curious, I suppose."

"Just curious?"

"I don't know," said Kline. He ran the edge of his stump along the grain of the table. It felt so good he did it again.

"What did Borchert have to say?" Ramse asked.

"A great guy, Borchert."

"You shouldn't make fun."

"Who says I'm making fun? He told me not to talk about it."

"I'm an eight, aren't I? You can talk to me. You don't have to keep a secret from me."

Kline shook his head, smiled. "It's not secret, it's sacred," he said.

"You shouldn't make fun," Ramse said again. "You should tolerate other peoples' religious beliefs. Besides, I already know a few things about it."

"Oh?" said Kline. "Why don't you tell me what you know?"

"Tit for tat," said Ramse. He slashed his stump bluntly past his face. "My lips are sealed," he said. "Besides, I've come on an errand. I'm supposed to conduct you to the scene of the crime."

The crime scene was in the same building that Borchert had been in. Ramse tried to follow Kline up but the guard instead locked Ramse outside on the porch, led Kline up alone.

"What do you know about this?" Kline asked.

"About what?" the guard asked.

"About the crime."

"What crime?"

"The murder."

"What murder?"

Kline stopped asking. On the third floor they passed the first and second doors, stopped at the third. The guard gestured to it.

"I'll wait here," he said.

"You don't care to come in?" asked Kline.

The guard said nothing. "Whose room is this?" asked Kline. The guard said nothing. "Aline's room?" asked Kline. The guard still said nothing.

"You're not allowed to come in?"

"I'll be waiting," said the guard. "Right here."

Kline sighed. Opening the door, he went in.

The room looked much like Borchert's room: a simple bed, a chair, a bare floor, little more. On the floor near the bed was a large irregular bloodstain, perhaps three times the size of Kline's head. The wall nearby was spattered with blood as well. Someone had drawn a figure in chalk on the floor, though it took Kline a moment to realize that was what it was.

"Good Christ," he said.

It looked like a simple blotch at first, but in a moment he realized what he was seeing was the outline of an armless and legless torso. He got down on his knees and looked more closely at the chalk figure. It must have been drawn wrong, for the head didn't fit snugly into the pool of dried blood that had sprent out of it. He got up, brushed off his knees, went over to look at the nearest wall. Blood was fanned all along it but in no regular pattern, as if spattered from eight or ten different blows. No blood on the other walls. It was as if the killer had struck the limbless torso once and then had hauled it a few feet away to strike it again, and so on. A legless, armless man wouldn't be able to cover much ground while being stabbed, would he?

He had stared at the wall for quite some time before it struck him that something else was wrong. He didn't have to bend over to see the spatter. He knelt down again beside the chalk torso and measured it roughly with his arm. It was slightly shorter than the arm itself. The spatter should be quite a bit lower on the wall.

Maybe, he thought, Aline had been in a chair. But the only chair in the room had no bloodstains on it. Maybe, he thought, whoever killed Aline had done so while holding him in their arms, perhaps dancing or spinning as he stabbed. He could imagine the limbless torso stiff, rigid, struggling.

But that didn't strike him as quite right either. True, he had been trained to infiltrate; true, his experience with crime scenes was far less than most of his former colleagues. Perhaps the killer had struck upward each time, as if carrying a golf swing through? Perhaps that would account for the odd spatter and the decreased amount of blood on the lower part of the wall?

But why? he wondered. Why strike that way at all?

And what was the instrument? From the way the spatter was slung he would have guessed a knife, some kind of blade. Without seeing a photograph of the body it was difficult to be sure. It hardly seemed likely that the killer would attempt to use a knife as if it were a golf club. Something was wrong.

He regarded the chalk torso, the way the blood had pooled unconvincingly out of the chalk head. It had been drawn wrong somehow. He reached out to touch the surface of the pool of dried blood. It looked almost lacquered. It was slick in some places, cracking on the surface in others, darker and thicker in the center. The light from the ceiling shined off it in a kind of busted nimbus, the shape not unlike that of a broken jaw.

What could blood tell? he wondered. *Where blood was could tell a lot. Could blood itself tell nothing?*

He got out his keys and dug at the blood in the center of the stain. The top quarter-inch layer cracked away in bits, but underneath it merely separated. Right near the floor the blood was almost moist, like a dough.

How long had it been? he wondered. They had started calling him several weeks ago. At least that; it could have been longer: he had been confused enough not to know exactly how much time had gone by. Aline, then, must have been dead for at least three weeks, perhaps more than a month. There was no way blood would stay moist for that long. It would either dry out completely or it would begin to rot and stink. And why were there no flies?

He went out into the hall. The guard was waiting, standing as stiffly as he had been when Kline had gone into the room.

"Nobody was killed in that room," said Kline

"I don't know what you're talking about," said the guard.

"Whose room is it?"

The guard just looked at him.

"I need to see Borchert," said Kline. "Right now."

"The room, Mr. Kline?" said Borchert absently. "What room is that exactly?" He held his mutilated finger between them and scrutinized it, his eyes flashing back and forth between it and Kline. "Nice work, don't you think, Mr. Kline?"

The fingertip was pale and puffy, streaked dark at the end, a sort of red collar just below the cut.

"It's infected," said Kline.

"Nonsense," said Borchert. "What you see is simply the body sealing itself off."

"About the room—"

"I can see the appeal of self-cauterization, Mr. Kline," said Borchert. "Ugly, true, but you really do have something there. Less clinical. A return to natural religion, so to speak."

"I don't have anything," said Kline. "This has nothing to do with me."

"Oh, but it does, Mr. Kline. You may be an unintentional avatar, but you are an avatar nonetheless."

"Look," said Kline. "I'm done with this. I'm leaving."

"So sorry, Mr. Kline," said Borchert. "But we've talked about this. If you try to leave, you'll be killed. Now what was this about the room?"

Kline shook his head. "Nobody was killed in that room."

"What room?"

"The murder room."

"Oh," said Borchert. "I see." He used his arm to raise himself out of the chair and onto his remaining leg and then stood there, half gone. He stood tilted slightly in the direction of his absent limbs, as if crimped at the side, for balance. "How can you be so sure, Mr. Kline?"

"Everything is wrong," said Kline. "The blood spatter pattern is irregular, the positioning of the body isn't right in regard to blood flow—"

"But surely, Mr. Kline, irregular doesn't mean falsified. Perhaps it's simply an unusual circumstance."

"Perhaps," said Kline. "But there's something wrong with the blood."

"The blood?"

"It isn't completely dry."

"But surely—"

"It's been artificially dried. A fan or a hair dryer or something. But it's still damp underneath. It couldn't possibly belong to the body of a man killed several weeks ago."

Borchert looked at him thoughtfully a long moment and slowly hopped his way around so he could slide back into the chair.

"Well?" said Kline.

"So it's a reconstruction," said Borchert. "So what?"

"So what?" said Kline. "How can I be expected to solve a crime by looking at a reconstruction of it?"

"Mr. Kline, surely you're enough of an armchair philosopher to realize that everything is a reconstruction of something else? Reality is a desperate and evasive creature."

"Am I being asked to solve the crime or the reconstruction of the crime?"

"The crime," said Borchert. "The reconstruction," he said, gesturing to himself with his thumb and his one and two-thirds fingers, "*c'est moi.*"

"I can't get anywhere without real evidence."

"I have perfect faith in you, Mr. Kline."

"At least let me talk to a few people who might know something."

"Somewhat tricky," said Borchert. "But, ever the optimist, I'm convinced something can be arranged."

Shaking his head, Kline went toward the door. Once there he turned, saw Borchert smiling in his chair. When he smiled, Kline realized that all his bottom teeth had been removed.

"This is going well, don't you think?" said Borchert, speaking loudly, perhaps for the sake of the guard. "Thank you, dear friend, for stopping by."

V.

Ramse showed up a few days later with a tape recorder balanced on his forearms. He put it on the table near Kline.

"What's this for?" asked Kline.

"It's a tape recorder," said Ramse. "For taping things. Borchert asked me to bring it."

"What does he want me to do with it?"

"It's for the interviews," said Ramse. "For the crime."

Kline nodded. He went to the fridge and poured himself a glass of milk, drank it slowly as Ramse watched.

"Anything else you need?" Kline asked.

"No," said Ramse. "Just that."

Kline nodded. "Right," he said. "Where's Gous?"

"He's getting ready for the party."

"The party?"

"Didn't he send you an invitation?"

"No."

Ramse furrowed his brow. "An oversight," he said. "He'd want you to come. I'm sure he wants you to come. Will you?"

Kline shrugged. "Why not?" he said.

"It's settled then," said Ramse. "I'll pick you up at eight."

Kline nodded, looked absently at his watch. Until the accident, he had worn his watch on his right arm, but now if he wore it there it threatened to slide off the stump.

Across the table, Ramse cleared his throat.

"You're still here?" asked Kline.

"Shall I wait outside or would you rather I came back later?" asked Ramse.

"For the party?"

"You don't understand," claimed Ramse. "I'm supposed to take the tape back."

"But I haven't conducted any interviews yet."

"That's what the tape's for."

"Right," said Kline. "To tape the interviews."

"No," said Ramse. "To tape the questions."

"To tape the questions?"

Ramse nodded. "These people," he said. "They're all ten or above. You're a one. You can't see them in person."

"But I see Borchert."

"Borchert's the exception," said Ramse. "You see him when someone above a ten has to be seen. If you were a three or a four some might condescend to see you, but they won't see a one. Not even a self-cauterizer."

"Jesus," said Kline. "That's ridiculous."

"I've been instructed by Borchert not to listen to the questions," said Ramse. "I'm only an eight. I don't need to know everything. I'm to take the tape back to Borchert once you've finished recording. Would you like me to wait in the hall or would you prefer I come back later?"

He sat staring at the tape recorder. It was ridiculous, he knew. Perhaps Ramse was right, it was only a question of proper behavior, no ones among the tens, but why in that case even bring him in at all? Why not solve their murder on their own?

He went and opened the door. Ramse was there, waiting, leaning against the wall. Kline closed the door again.

What were his options? One: he could refuse to send the tape back. Borchert would hardly allow that. He would be punished in some way, he was certain. And it would only prolong the amount of time he would have to spend in the compound. Two: he could send back a blank tape. Same problem: it bought him a little time, but time for what? Three: he could send back a series of questions. That had the advantage of moving things forward, or at least of moving them in some direction.

He sighed. He went to the table and pressed the record button.

"One: State your name and your relation to the deceased.

"Two: Where were you on the night Aline was murdered?

"Three: Do you know of anyone who might want Aline dead for any reason?

"Four: Did you see the body? If so, please describe in detail what you saw.

"Five: Are you absolutely certain Aline's death wasn't a suicide?

"Six: Did you kill Aline?"

It was ridiculous, but at least it was a start. They would tell him nothing, he was almost sure. He turned the tape off.

Ramse showed up at eight o'clock sharp, wearing a tuxedo that had been modified to better reveal his amputations, no shoes, no socks. He had, slung over one arm, a plastic dry cleaner's bag containing another tuxedo, which he handed to Kline.

"Try this on," he said.

Kline did. It was a little loose but generally fit quite well, the right sleeve cut back slightly to reveal his stump.

They walked across the gravel lot in front of the house, following the road toward the gate, turning down a footpath after about a hundred meters. At the end was a gravel circle, a bar to the left, a neon one-legged woman on the sign. A well-lit lodge structure was to the right, which was where they went.

A one-handed man was standing at the open door, smiling. Kline could hear music blaring from the door behind him.

"Hello, Ramse," the man said affably. "This the guy?"

"This is him, John," said Ramse. "In the flesh."

They both laughed at that for some reason. The man held out his remaining hand, his right. "Put it there," he said, which Kline tried, left-handed and very awkwardly, to do.

"Self-cauterizer, huh?" asked John. "People have been talking. There's a buzz going."

"Don't embarrass him, John," said Ramse. Ushering Kline before him, he made his way in.

The room was filled with several dozen men in tuxedos, all amputees. Streamers descended without pattern from the ceiling, brushing against men's shoulders, dipping into their drinks. Ramse took him to the bar and Kline got a drink and stood next to Ramse nursing it, giving Ramse sips from time to time. The men were mostly ones or twos as far as Kline could tell in the dim light, though there were fours and fives as well and one person that Kline thought might be a seven or eight—the room was dark and in motion so it was hard to tell how many toes the man was actually missing. Then suddenly Gous was beside him, rubbing his shoulder with his stump.

"How nice of you to come," he said to Kline, smiling. He was dressed differently than the others. He was wearing a tuxedo, but one sleeve of it had been wrapped in plastic, and a line had been drawn in permanent marker between his middle and fourth finger, angling across his palm to terminate at the palm's edge just before the wrist. "Ramse didn't know if you'd come," he said, "but I was sure you would." He turned to Ramse. "Stretter didn't come, the bastard."

"I'm sure he meant to," said Ramse. "Something must have come up."

"No," said Gous. "He never meant to. I came for him three times, but now that he's a five, he's too good for me."

"Surely he can't mean it personally," said Ramse. "It's just some sort of mistake."

But Gous was already turning away, shaking his head. Kline watched Ramse go after him. He took a sip of his drink, looked around, then began to walk slowly around the room. There were no women, he quickly realized, nothing but men, everyone in their thirties and forties, nobody either very young or very old.

The back of the room wasn't a solid wall at all but a divider, a series of linked panels that, he saw, looking more closely, slid along a metal track in the floor. The two central panels each had a handle and a latch holding them together.

"Would you like to have a look?" asked a voice behind him.

"Where are all the women?" asked Kline, turning. Behind him was John.

"Aren't any here," said John, smiling. "There are a few over in the bar, but otherwise none. This is a brotherhood, after all."

Kline nodded, looked about him.

"So, you want a preview?" asked John.

Kline shrugged.

"I don't think anyone would mind," John said. "They've all seen it before anyway."

He put his drink down on the floor, used his hand to turn one of the latches. The panel disengaged and slid open an inch. He rolled it along the track until there was enough space for Kline to slide through.

"Go on," he said, stooping for his drink. "I'll wait out here."

Kline slid through, careful not to spill his drink. On the other side, the remainder of the hall was dark and bare and sober except for a rolling metal table draped in white cloth. A smaller square table, also draped in cloth, sat beside it. A large domed light was over them. It was the only light in the room, the dome functioning like a spotlight.

He smelled the smoke before he saw the man step out of the darkness and move toward him. The man was wearing scrubs, had his cloth surgical mask pulled down around his neck so he could smoke a cigarette. When he lifted the cigarette to his lips, Kline could see he was missing a finger.

"Is it time?" he asked. And then, seeing the drink in Kline's hand, "Are you bringing that for me?"

Kline handed him the drink, and without a word left.

"Well," said John. "What do you think? First-rate setup, no?"

"Where's Ramse?" asked Kline.

"Ramse?" said John. "I don't know," he said. "Maybe over there?"

Kline started across the hall, moving from cluster to cluster until he found Ramse speaking to a man in a chair whose legs had been cut off at the knee.

"I need to talk to you," he said.

"All right," said Ramse, excusing himself from the legless man. "What's the trouble?"

"Jesus," said Kline. "What kind of party is this?"

"It's Gous' party," said Ramse. "His three. Where's your drink? Do you need another drink?"

"What the hell does that mean?"

"Isn't it obvious?" said Ramse. He looked at Kline, eyes wide, then shook his head. "I forget you don't know us very well," he said. "It's an amputation party."

"An amputation party."

"Like a coming out," said Ramse. "Gous is giving up two fingers. He's gathered his friends around him for the occasion. He's going from a one to a three."

"Jesus," said Kline. "I have to leave."

Kline tried to make for the door but Ramse was pressing his forearm to Kline's chest. "You can't leave," hissed Ramse, "not now that you've come. It'd break Gous' heart."

"But," said Kline. "I don't believe in any of this. I can't stay here."

"It's not that you don't believe," said Ramse. "It's just that you don't have the call yet."

"No," said Kline. "It's that I don't believe."

"I don't care what you believe," said Ramse. "Just do this for Gous. He admires you. What has he ever done to you to deserve this?"

"What has he ever done to deserve losing his fingers?"

"He doesn't see it that way," said Ramse. "He's had the call. This for him is an act of faith. You don't have to believe in it, but you can still respect him."

"I have to go," said Kline, pushing against his arm.

"No," said Ramse. "Please, just for Gous. Have compassion. Please."

By the time the amputation took place, Kline had had a few drinks, had drunk enough in fact that he had trouble making his eyes focus. To see reasonably well, he had to cover one eye with his stump.

Eventually Ramse coaxed the drink out of his hand, goaded him now through the open partition and into the half-room beyond. He stood on the edge of the lit circle, swaying slightly, Ramse beside him, Ramse's forearm tucked under his arm. In the center was the doctor, his mask up now. He had stripped the cloth off the small metal cart to reveal an array of tools that seemed half to be medical instruments, half to be from the knife block of a gourmet chef. *Jesus*, Kline thought.

Gous came into the circle, smiling, while the tuxedo-dressed gentlemen clapped gently. Two gentlemen were called forward as witnesses, each of them placing a stump under one of Gous' arms. He leaned over the large table, placed his hand on it, palm up. The doctor took a hypodermic off the table and slid its needle into Kline's hand. His fingers twitched. Or rather *Gous'* fingers, Kline realized; it was not his own hand, he could not start to think of it as his own hand. The four of them—the doctor, Gous, the two witnesses—stood as if in tableau, motionless in a way that Kline found unbearable, only the doctor moving from time to time to regard his watch. At last he took a metal probe from the small metal cart and pushed at the hand.

Gous watched him, then nodded slightly. The two witnesses braced themselves behind him. The doctor switched on a cauterizer. After a moment, Kline could smell the way it oxidized the air. The doctor let his fingers run over the instruments, then took up the cauterizer with one hand. What looked like a stylized and carefully balanced cleaver was in the other. He approached the table, lined the cleaver along the line Gous had drawn on his hand, and then raised it, brought it swiftly down.

Kline saw Gous' eyelids flutter, then the rest of his body faltered and was supported and caught by the witnesses behind him. All around, the men began to clap quietly, and blood began to spurt from the wound. Kline closed his eyes, felt himself begin to lean to one side, but Ramse caught him, held him upright. He could hear the buzz of the cauterizer and a moment later began to smell burning flesh.

"Hey," whispered Ramse. "Are you all right?" All around them, men were beginning to move.

"Just a little drunk," said Kline, opening his eyes. Gous was there before him, having his hand bandaged.

"That wasn't so bad, was it?" asked Ramse. "Gous certainly didn't think so. Not so bad, eh?"

"I don't know," Kline said. "I want to go home."

"The night's still young," said Ramse. "We're only getting started."

The rest of the night was a blur to him. At some point he lost his tuxedo jacket; at another point, he found the next day, someone had smeared a swath of blood across his forehead. At one point he could hear Ramse telling everyone not to give him another drink and then he was outside, vomiting onto the gravel, Ramse seeming to be trying at once to hold him up and to knock him over. Then they were stumbling across the gravel courtyard, Kline covering one of his eyes so he could see, and into the bar where he was drinking not whiskey but first coffee and then water. It was not exactly a bar either, but more like a club. They were sitting in armchairs, a small coffee table before them, pointed toward a stage, and Kline realized the curtain was opening.

The stage was bare at first, lit by a reddish spotlight, and then a woman came out onto it swaddled from knees to neck in boas.

"Watch this," said Ramse, his words slurring even more than usual. "She's really something."

A strip show, thought Kline. He had seen a strip show before, more than once, had seen several in fact with the man who had since come to be known as the gentleman with the cleaver, the man who was dead now. He didn't care about strip shows one way or the other. He watched the woman lose one boa after another while Ramse whistled. She would let a boa trail first and then finally let it flop all the way off and then kick it to one side of the stage. And then finally she was done, stripped naked, blurred in the red light, not particularly attractive.

He waited for the curtain to go down but the curtain did not go down. He turned to Ramse but found him still staring rapt at the girl, and so he himself turned back to her and watched as, with a flick of the wrist, she cracked off her hand.

A dim howl went up through the house and Kline heard, scattered through the chairs, a dull thumping, the sound of stumps beating against one another. She made her way toward one side of the stage, spinning slightly, and then snapped the stump of her arm against her remaining hand and Kline saw three fingers wobble loose and slough away. The crowd roared. He tried to stand up but Ramse had his hand on his shoulder and was shouting in his ear. "Just wait," Ramse shouted, "the best is yet to come!"

And then the woman sashayed across the stage and reached up with her remaining finger and thumb to tear free her ear. She spun it around a few times before tossing it out into the audience. Kline saw a group of men rise up in a dark mass, trying somehow, with what hands they had left between them, to catch it. And then she turned away, turned her back to them, and when she turned back her artificial breasts had been pulled away to hang like an apron around her belly, revealing two shiny flat patches where they had been. She spread her legs and squatted and Kline imagined her legs were beginning to separate, to split up. *Jesus, God*, he thought, and tried to stand, and felt Ramse trying to hold him down, and felt the blood rush to his head. He staggered forward and into the small table, hot coffee sloshing all over his legs, and looked up to see the woman on the stage gouging her fingers beneath one side of her face, but mercifully, before she had torn it away, he had fallen and did not, despite Ramse's urging, get up again.

VI.

It was late in the afternoon before he could bring himself to get up again, his head still spinning. He went into the bathroom and drank cup after cup of water and then turned on the shower, stood under the nozzle for a while, steam rising around him.

He got dressed and opened the door, found outside a covered plate of food and, next to it, a cassette tape. Putting the plate of food on the table, he removed the lid. Pancakes, sodden now with syrup, with eggs floating grimly to one side. There was no silverware. He ate with his fingers until he felt sick, then went to the bathroom and threw up and then came back and ate a little more, just enough to keep something in his stomach.

The tape he put into the tape recorder, turned it on.

"One: State your name and your relation to the deceased," he heard himself asking.

"Two: Where were you on the night Aline was murdered?

"Three: Do you know of anyone who might want Aline dead for any reason?

"Four: Did you see the body? If so, please describe in detail what you saw.

"Five: Are you absolutely certain Aline's death wasn't a suicide?

"Six: Did you kill Aline?"

What followed was a blank unrolling of tape, a dim static that lasted five or six minutes, and then the tape clicked loudly and a man's voice began to talk.

"Helming," the voice said. "We were . . . associates." There was a pause, the tape microphone clicked off but the tape ran on.

"I was in my room. I heard a noise and had Michael carry me out into the hall and—"

The tape fell suddenly silent, part of it erased.

"I don't know why anyone would [blank space] question I suppose of having insufficient faith."

"No, I didn't see the [blank] . . ."

"Yes."

"No. I—"

The tape cut abruptly off, and there was silence and then it resumed with another voice, another individual, the same enigmatic, half-erased style, nothing really stated of substance. Why were there gaps? A third voice was the same, and it was only then that Kline realized that the answers being given were vague enough that they could be read as responses to almost any questions. *On that night I was in my room. I heard a noise and went into the hall and—* could be answering his question *Where were you on the night Aline was killed?* but he could imagine other questions that might have been posed that would elicit the same response. *Where were you on the night the hallway was graffitied? Where were you on the night Marker came in drunk?* None of the three recorded voices mentioned the word "murdered" or the word "Aline" or the word "death." Or if they did it was in the portion of the tape that had been erased.

He rewound the tape and listened again, turning up the volume as high as it would go, listening to the blank spots of erased tape, hoping to hear hints of whatever had been there before the erasure. He heard nothing but a low half-muttering which, he realized, wasn't a human voice at all but the magnified sound of the tape recorder's mechanism itself. He turned off the tape and sat, thinking, wondering what to do next.

When Ramse arrived with dinner balanced on his arms in the early evening, Kline demanded to see Borchert.

"I'll put in a request," said Ramse.

"I need to see him right away," said Kline. "I need to see him now."

"Right now what you need to do is eat some supper," said Ramse. "And try to get over your hangover. You were a hell of a mess last night."

"I need to see Borchert," said Kline. "It's urgent."

"Fine," said Ramse. "Go ahead and eat. I'll walk over and see what I can do."

At the door he stopped and looked back, a look of reproach on his face. "You didn't even ask about Gous," he said.

"What about him?"

"About how he's doing."

"How is he doing?"

"Good," said Ramse. "He's doing just fine."

"Wonderful," said Kline. "Now, goddammit, go get Borchert."

Once Ramse was gone Kline uncovered the tray and ate: boiled potatoes, a thin and curling piece of grayish meat, a pile of overcooked carrots. He ate slowly, moving from potatoes to meat to carrots and back again until it was all gone, then sat playing the tape over. It seemed obvious that there was no real interest in solving the crime. *Why even bring me out at all?*

When Ramse returned, he turned the tape off.

"It's all arranged," said Ramse. "Borchert will see you."

"Good," said Kline, standing up. "Let's go."

Ramse looked a little surprised. "Oh, not today, Mr. Kline," he said. "He can't do it today."

"I need to see him today."

"He can see you in three days," said Ramse. "That was the best he could do."

Kline pushed past Ramse and went out the door, out of the house. He could hear Ramse calling after him, loudly. He walked briskly across the gravel-ridden lot in front of the house, turned down the road, cut at the right moment down the path to dip down through the trees. He wondered if Ramse was following him. He broke into a jog.

He came up over the top, the tree-lined path, the house looming up, the gate before it, a guard darting out again from behind a pillar of the house, standing at the far side of the gate regarding him with one eye. He couldn't tell if it was the same guard as before.

"What is wanted?" asked the guard.

"I'm here to see Borchert," said Kline, moving forward until he was nearly touching the gate.

"Borchert isn't seeing anyone today," said the guard.

"He'll see me."

The guard swiveled his head a little, fixed his remaining eye hard on Kline. "No," he said. "He won't."

Kline reached across the top of the gate and punched him. He was prepared to feel his hand strike the guard's temple but the sensation of his stump striking it was an odd one. It ached. The guard fell to the ground without a word, and as he struggled to get up Kline clambered over the gate. He kicked him a few times until he was sure the guard had stopped moving.

By the time he was knocking on the door of the house, he could see Ramse nearing the gate. The gatekeeper was still down but on his knees now, struggling his way up. He knocked again and the inner guard cracked the door open and said "What is wanted?" and Kline, without awaiting a response, kicked the door hard so that the edge of it split open the man's forehead and he stumbled back, spattering blood. Kline struck him open-palmed on the chest, knocking him down, and rushed by, down the hall and into the stairwell.

But before he had made the third floor he was struck hard on the back of the head. A stair tread rose up and struck his face. By the time he got up, there were one-eyed men all around him, and his own blood was getting into his eyes. Then they were hitting him so hard and so often that he could no longer hear, or rather what sound there was came in waves, and it seemed that he was falling down more stairs than there were stairs to fall down, and then, after that, he had a hard time even remembering that he was human.

When his eyes focused again, there was Borchert, above him. He realized he was lying on the floor of Borchert's room, blood coming in phlegm-streaked ribbons from his nose. He pulled himself up to sitting, wiped his arm across his face.

"Well, Mr. Kline," said Borchert. "It seems you wanted to see me quite badly."

Kline said nothing.

"What is this all about?"

He tried to speak but before he could get anything out had to swallow back blood.

"Was it worth it, Mr. Kline?" asked Borchert. "It was once such a lovely face, too. Are you willing to trade your face for a little face-to-face conversation?"

"I need to see them," said Kline.

"Them?" asked Borchert. "My dear Kline, who?"

"The people on the tape."

"Mr. Kline," said Borchert. "You're a one. You can hardly expect someone in the double digits—"

"I need to see them," said Kline.

"But Mr. Kline—"

"Something's wrong with the tape," said Kline. "With the questions. It doesn't all mesh."

Borchert looked at him, coolly. "I don't think that you should let the tape trouble you, Mr. Kline. Why don't you simply accept it for what it purports to be?"

"Because it's not what it is," said Kline.

Borchert nodded slowly. "Very well, Mr. Kline," he said. "What do you propose?"

"I need to see them," Kline said. "Rules or no."

"And you want me to make the necessary arrangements. You're certain of it?"

"Yes," said Kline.

Borchert sighed. "So be it," he said. "I'll make the necessary arrangements, Mr. Kline. You'll see them tomorrow."

"I want to see them today."

"Not today, tomorrow. Don't push your luck."

Kline nodded, stood to go. His body was sore, bruised.

"Would you mind wiping your blood off the floor before you go, Mr. Kline?" asked Borchert, rising from the chair to stand perfectly balanced on his remaining leg. "And Mr. Kline," he said. "Now you have a history of violence. I advise you to be careful."

◆ ◆ ◆

Late evening, Gous arrived with a half-empty bottle of Scotch cradled in the crook of his elbow, Scotch which was, according to him, *compliments of Borchert.*

"How kind of him," said Kline, flatly.

"Why he should care after your escapade this afternoon is beyond me," said Gous.

"Maybe that's why I only get half a bottle."

Gous nodded. "Do you have glasses?" he asked.

"No."

"I guess Borchert didn't think you rated glasses," said Gous. He fumbled awkwardly at the lid with his bandaged hand. "I'm going to have to ask you to open it," he said.

"How's your hand?" asked Kline.

"Nice of you to ask," said Gous. "Recovering nicely, thank you," he said, lifting the bandaged lump in the air. "I'm supposed to keep it elevated. And I shouldn't drink too much," he said. "Alcohol thins the blood and all that."

Kline screwed the cap off the bottle and drank. It was good Scotch, or at least good enough. He took another mouthful then pushed the bottle over to Gous, who, using his forearms like chopsticks, managed to get it to his mouth. He almost upset the bottle putting it back on the table.

"What made you change your mind?" he asked.

"My mind?" asked Kline.

"About amputation."

"Who said I changed my mind?" Lifting the bottle, he took another drink.

"Why would Borchert have sent over a bottle otherwise? Did you get a call?"

"I don't know what you're talking about."

Gous nodded. "It's nobody's business but your own," he said.

Kline reached for the bottle, watched the stump at the end of his arm knock against it, nearly knock it over. "Nobody's business but my own," he said, aloud, his voice sounding quite distant.

"That's right," Gous said. "That's what *I* said."

Kline could see on the end of his arm, the ghost of his hand, pale and transparent, sprouting oddly from the stump. "That's right," he heard himself say. He flexed his missing fingers, saw them move. They had cut off his hand but the ghost of his hand was still there. Perhaps this was what was meant by a call? Perhaps Borchert, shorn of most of his limbs, saw the ghosts of what was missing: vanished limbs grown uncarnate, pure.

He looked up. There was Gous, across the table from him, his eyes drooping, half-closed, his face mostly gone in shadow. Kline tried to reach for the bottle but couldn't find it.

"Where was I?" he asked.

He saw Gous' eyelids wince, come all the way open. "We should get you into bed," Gous said. "While I still can."

"It isn't Scotch," said Kline, to where Gous had been, but Gous wasn't there anymore. It took him some time to realize that Gous was there beside him, looming above him, trying to get him out of the chair. And then, without knowing how, he was standing, Gous beside him, and they were gliding slowly through the room.

"No," said Gous, slowly. "It *is* Scotch. But that's not all it is."

Fuck, thought Kline. "I thought you were my friend," he said, and felt himself falling. And then he was on the bed, sprawled, Gous sitting beside him looking down at him.

"I am your friend," Gous said. "I drank with you, didn't I?"

Kline tried to nod but nothing happened. He could see the wrappings around Gous' hand staining with blood.

"Besides," said Gous, "friendship is one thing, God another."

"Scoot over," Gous said. Kline was not sure how much time had passed. "There's enough room on that bed for two."

Gous' cheek on the pillow, just next to his own eye, was the last thing he would remember until, hours later, he awoke, alone, to the sight of his bandaged foot, the bandages already steeped with blood. Even then it was not until he felt the dressings with his remaining hand that he realized that three of his toes had been removed.

VII.

"This is what you wanted," said Borchert after Kline had forced his shoe over his bandaged foot and limped over to Borchert's building. It had been difficult to walk without the toes, hard to keep his balance, and very painful. By the time he had reached the building his shoe was saturated with blood. The guard, perhaps the same guard as the day before, had regarded him with one eye and said, "What is wanted?" In answer he had merely lifted his bloody shoe slightly. The guard, without another word, let him pass, as did the guard behind the door. And now here he was, upstairs, across from Borchert, in Borchert's room, being told that he had gotten what he wanted.

"You should be careful about what you ask for," said Borchert.

"I didn't ask for anything."

"You asked," said Borchert, "to interview certain people in person. I told you I would make arrangements. I have made them. I took the fewest number of toes possible," he said. "Even now, for them to see you is to stretch the rules a little. A four, normally . . . but it isn't unheard of."

"I want to leave," said Kline.

"Of course you do," said Borchert cheerily. "But I believe we've already discussed that. It's not possible."

"Why are you doing this?"

"What am I doing exactly?" asked Borchert. "I've made you a four. I've done you a favor."

"I don't see it that way."

"Perhaps someday you will."

"I doubt it."

Borchert looked at him seriously. "I doubt it too," he said. "Look," he said, "at your missing hand."

"When can I leave?" asked Kline.

"When all this is done."

"When will that be?"

Borchert shrugged. "That depends on you," he said. He lifted his remaining hand, pointed his crippled middle digit at Kline. "Now, if I'm not mistaken, you have interviews to conduct."

He was taken down a floor and then down the hall to another door, behind which was one of the interviewees, an eleven, his legs hacked off at the knees, his fingers and one thumb all shaved down nearly to knuckle. He recognized his voice as the third on the tape: Andreissen. Before he would speak with Kline, Andreissen demanded to see the missing toes, suggesting that Kline should not *hide his light under a bushel*.

Kline sat and loosened his shoe and slowly worked it off, blood dripping from it to puddle on the floor. He dropped the shoe onto the floor and began unwrapping the sodden dressing. Andreissen came nimbly out of his chair and, like an ape, propelled himself across the floor on his knuckles and the stumps of his knees. His eyes were lucid and shining, and when Kline got the wrapping off to reveal his mangled foot Andreissen came very close indeed. Kline could hardly bear to look at the foot. The place where the toes had been was cauterized but now cracked and seeping a flux of blood and pus.

"I thought you self-cauterized," said Andreissen. "Part of the reason I agreed to this was because I wanted to see what self-cauterization looked like."

"I didn't do this," said Kline.

"You shouldn't be walking on it," he said. "Doesn't it hurt?"

"Of course it hurts."

Andreissen nodded. He knuckled his way back across the floor, clambered back into the chair. "As I told Borchert," he said, once properly situated, "I'm here to help. I'm all for law and order."

"Good for you," said Kline.

"But, honestly, I said all there was to say on the tape."

Kline nodded. He dragged his foot along the floor, watching the thin lines of blood run. "It's about the tape," he said. "That's what I came about."

"Oh?"

"There's something wrong with the tape," said Kline. "I need to figure out what."

"The tape didn't work?"

"Something like that," said Kline. "So I'm just going to ask the questions again, all right?"

"Why don't you talk to Borchert?" he asked. "Why don't you ask him?"

"First question," said Kline. "State your name and your relation to the deceased."

"Technically that's not a question."

"Please answer," said Kline.

"I believe you already know my name," he said. "It's Andreissen."

"Thank you," said Kline. "What was your relation to the deceased?"

"The deceased?" said Andreissen. "I thought you were sticking to the original questions."

"That is one of the original questions."

"No it isn't."

"It's not?" said Kline.

"What's this talk of the deceased? There is no deceased."

"Aline."

"What about Aline?"

"He's the deceased."

"Aline?" Andreissen shook his head, laughed. "You're pulling my leg."

"Aline's dead."

"It's impossible," said Andreissen.

"Why do you think I'm here?"

"I saw him just yesterday," said Andreissen. "He seemed very much alive to me."

"You're lying," said Kline.

"I swear to you," said Andreissen. "On my missing legs."

Kline stood, limped around the room.

"Can you stop that?" said Andreissen. "You're getting blood everywhere."

"What were the questions you were asked? On the tape, what were the questions?"

"Me? About the robbery of course."

"What robbery?"

Andreissen narrowed his eyes. "What is this all about? Do you think I did it? I didn't do it."

"Do what?"

"The robbery."

"What robbery?"

"Christ," said Andreissen. "What sort of game are you playing?"

"Where's Aline's room? Down the hall?"

"No," said Andreissen. "Up a level. Last door. Why?"

"I was told it was somewhere else."

"What is this?" asked Andreissen. He posted his palms against the chair's arms, pulled himself up to stand in the chair's seat on his stumps. "I didn't agree to this. Borchert didn't say anything about this. I want you to leave."

"Fine," said Kline. "I'm leaving."

He went out into the hall. The guard was gone. He went to the stairs but instead of going down went up and down to the end of the hall. A guard was standing in front of the last door. He watched Kline nervously.

"This is Aline's room?" Kline asked.

The guard made no gesture, said nothing.

"Mind if I see for myself?" asked Kline, and reached for the doorknob.

The guard struck him once with the edge of his palm, fast, in the throat. He couldn't breathe. He stumbled back, his hand to his throat, still unable to breathe, and then made a conscious decision to stumble forward instead, throwing himself against the door. The handle was locked. The guard hit him again, in the side of the temple, and he slid down along the door, and then the guard was pulling him back into the middle of the hall, massaging his throat, trying to help him to breathe again.

◆◆◆

"Well," said Borchert. "Mr. Kline. Always a pleasant surprise. You should be more careful. You should have a little more respect."

"Aline's not dead," said Kline, still rubbing his throat.

"Of course he is," said Borchert. "Whatever gave you that idea?"

"Andreissen."

"Why would he say that?" asked Borchert.

"He said I was here to investigate a robbery."

"No, no," said Borchert. "Aline's dead. You're here for Aline."

"Who's dead?"

"It's that you're only a four," said Borchert. "He's not telling you the truth because of that."

"You're lying."

"Maybe we should remove another toe," said Borchert. "Or maybe two more. Then we'll see if Andreissen tells you the truth."

"No," said Kline. "No more toes."

"All right, then," said Borchert. "Perhaps one of the others will be a little more forthcoming."

"No more interviews."

"All right," said Borchert. "You're the investigator. You should do what feels right."

Using his remaining foot, Borchert pushed the chair slowly along the floor until he was back by the counter. Slowly he managed to open the cabinet above it and to tug down first one glass and then another. And then, more precariously, a bottle of Scotch. He took off the cap with his mouth. He moved the glasses to the edge of the counter and, pinning the bottle between his arm and his body, poured.

"Drink?" he asked.

"Absolutely not," said Kline.

"Oh come on," said Borchert. "It's Scotch, plain and simple. Nothing but Scotch."

"No," said Kline.

"Suit yourself," said Borchert. He pinched the glass' rim between his thumb and remaining half-finger, lifted it to his lips, drank. "So," he said. "Made any progress, have we?"

"On what?"

"On finding Aline's killer."

"My guess is that Aline is still very much alive."

"Please, Mr. Kline. Let's have no more such talk."

"Show me the body."

Borchert shook his head. "I can't allow you to see the body. At the very least you'd have to lose a few more toes."

"This is absurd."

"Be that as it may, Mr. Kline," said Borchert, taking a large swallow. "Be that as it may."

Later that evening he wandered out of his room and down the hall and into the gravel yard in front of the building. He stood looking up at the stars, his foot aching with pain, feeling slightly feverish. He did not understand what it was he had gotten himself into, nor for that matter how he had gotten himself into it. But the more important question was, now that he was in, how to get out.

He walked out to the main road, turned, limped toward the main gates. A man was dead, murdered, or perhaps very much alive. Borchert was playing with him, and perhaps the others were as well. The night was cool, cloudless. Where was this place? He turned and looked back, saw the building he was staying in, the only light being that of his own room. Why was nobody else in the building? Had there been anyone living in the building but him since his arrival? Where did Gous and Ramse sleep?

At the main gate at the edge of the compound, the guard stepped out of the shadows and flicked on his flashlight, shining the beam into Kline's eyes.

"What is wanted?" he asked.

"It's Kline," Kline said, squinting his eyes.

"Right," said the guard. "We met the first night. A one. Self-cauterizer. Right hand, right?"

"Yes," said Kline. "Now a four."

"A four?" said the guard. "That was quick. What else?"

"A few toes," he said. "Nothing much."

The guard moved the flashbeam down, shined it on Kline's feet. Kline could see the man now, a dim shape just behind the flashlight.

"I need to leave," said Kline. "Please open the gate."

"I'm sorry," said the guard. "I can't do that."

"My work here is finished," said Kline.

"I have my orders, I'm afraid," said the guard.

Kline took a step forward. The guard brought the light up and into his eyes. Kline took another step and heard a rustling and a click and the guard quickly flashed the light back on himself to reveal a sort of metal prosthetic slipped over his stump, a gun barrel at the end of it.

"I thought prosthetics were frowned upon," said Kline.

"We don't like to use them," said the guard. "But when we have to, we do."

"Say I climb the fence somewhere."

"You're welcome to try. My guess is we'd catch you eventually."

Kline nodded, turned to leave.

"Very nice to see you, Mr. Kline," said the guard. "If you have any more questions, don't hesitate to ask."

He found Gous and Ramse in the bar, already drunk, Ramse in particular, who was drinking whiskey through a straw. Gous kept saying he had to go easy, that it thinned the blood, and then taking another drink. They cheered when they caught sight of Kline, clapped him on the back with their stumps.

"Drink?" asked Ramse.

Kline nodded. Ramse called the bartender over. "A drink for my friend here," he said.

"The self-cauterizer."

"Word gets around," said Ramse.

"Say," said Gous, his voice slurred and too slow. "When do the women come out?"

"Ten," said the bartender. "I told you already. Ten."

"Drink?" Ramse asked Kline.

"He's already getting me a drink," said Kline.

"Hell," said Ramse. "I wanted to get you a drink."

"You did," said Kline.

"What?" asked Ramse. "What?"

"Never mind," said Kline.

"Just so you know," said Ramse. "I'm buying the next one."

Kline smiled.

"So," said Gous, hunched over his drink. "How's the investigation?"

"It's not."

"No?" said Gous. "Thash too bad."

"Do you want to hear about it?" asked Kline.

"About what?" asked Ramse.

"The investigation," said Kline. The bartender put the drink on the counter. Kline took it up in his left hand and drank from it.

"Oh, no," said Ramse. "You can't tell Gous anything."

"Why not?" asked Gous. "Why not?"

"Gous is a one," said Ramse. "We can't bring a one in."

"I was a one," said Kline. "They brought me in."

"I'm not a one," said Gous, lifting up his hand. "Not any more."

"Still," said Ramse. "You're not much. You're what you are and we love you for it, but you're not much."

"It's all right, Ramse," said Kline. "Trust me."

"I just don't think—"

"Ramse," said Kline. "Trust me and listen."

Ramse opened his mouth, then closed it again.

"Aline is dead," Kline said.

"Aline is dead?" said Ramse, his voice rising.

"Is that possible?" said Gous. "How is that possible?"

"Or not," said Kline. "Maybe not."

"Well," said Gous. "Which is it?"

"What did you say about Aline?" asked the bartender.

"Nothing," said Kline.

"Oh, God," said Ramse, shaking his head. "Dear God."

"Aline is either dead or not dead," said Gous to the bartender.

"Be quiet, Gous," said Kline.

"Well, which is he?" asked the bartender. "Dead or not dead? There's a big difference, you know."

"That," said Gous, stabbing the air with his stump. "Is what I intend to find out."

"You don't think there's a big difference?" asked Ramse.

"Ramse," said Kline. "Look at me. Why am I here? What am I investigating?"

"What?" said Ramse. "Smuggling."

"Smuggling?"

Gous, Kline noticed, was watching them more intently.

"Somebody smuggled out pictures."

"What sorts of pictures?"

"Sex pictures," said Ramse. "Of people missing limbs. Somebody stealing them and selling them without the proceeds benefiting the community."

"That," said Kline, "in your opinion, is why I am here?"

Ramse nodded.

"No," said Kline. "I'm here because of Aline."

"Who's either dead or not dead."

"Exactly," said Kline.

"There's a big difference," said Gous. "That's what we intend to find out."

"What?" said Ramse.

"That," said Gous.

"What?" said Ramse, looking around. "What's going on?"

"Exactly," said Kline. "That's what I want to know."

VIII.

There are two possibilities, he thought, as he was escorted on his way to visit Borchert the next morning, a hungover Ramse on one side of him, a hungover Gous on the other side. He was coming at Borchert's request. *Possibility one: Aline is dead. Possibility two: Aline is alive.* Perhaps Ramse was right, perhaps he really did know something and the reason he, Kline, was here was because of smuggling or theft. But if it was smuggling, why hadn't he been told? Why had Borchert told him he was investigating a murder? Certainly, considering what Kline's specialty had been before, it seemed more logical that they would recruit him to investigate a smuggling operation.

Perhaps Borchert himself had a vested interest, had reasons to stop the smuggling from being investigated.

But even so, why declare Aline dead? Why suggest there is a murder to be investigated? Why not simply suggest something a little more benign?

And here he was, standing alone in front of Borchert, with Gous and Ramse abandoned at the gate, the one-armed, one-legged man looking grimly at him from his chair.

"I thought we had an agreement," Borchert was saying.

"What agreement?"

"I asked you not to speak about the case with those who didn't need to know. Instead, you've been spreading rumors."

"Look," said Kline. "I don't know what I'm doing here. What exactly am I investigating?"

"Aline's death."

"I don't believe Aline is dead."

"No," said Borchert. "You've made that quite clear."

"What about the smuggling?"

"The smuggling," said Borchert. "A cover story. Something we agreed to tell people like Ramse."

"And Andreissen?"

"We talked about that," said Borchert. "I give my solemn word that if you simply have one or two more amputations, Andreissen will change his story. Why didn't you speak to any of the others? Perhaps one of them would tell you the truth."

"You're lying."

Borchert sighed. "Well," he said. "I was hoping it wouldn't come to this, but you're a stubborn bastard and have your own particular way of conducting business. You'd be better off if you were willing to take some things on faith, but *Thou woulds't doubt*, as Jesus said, and for the doubting there's nothing but what you can touch." He turned his head, gestured with his chin to the counter behind. "There's a gun there," he said. "In the drawer. No bullets in it, but the guard outside Aline's door doesn't need to know that. If you need to go see for yourself, go see for yourself. I wouldn't advise it, but neither will I prevent you."

Kline took the pistol and left. He could see, as soon as he opened the door to the hall, the guard in front of what he had been told by Andreissen was Aline's door. Was it the door Borchert expected him to go to as well? he wondered. Or was he being told to visit the room where Borchert had led him before, the faked crime scene?

"Is this the door to Aline's room?" Kline asked the guard.

The guard did not reply. Kline realized the man's lone eye was directed downward, fixed on his hand, and then Kline remembered the gun. He lifted his hand, pointed the pistol at the man's head.

"Please open the door," he said.

The guard shook his head.

"I'll kill you," said Kline.

"Then kill me."

Kline hit the guard hard in the face with his stump, then hit him across his jaw with the butt of the pistol. The guard took two awkward steps, wavering into the door, and Kline struck him with the pistol butt again, just behind the ear. The man went down in a heap.

The door was unlocked. He opened it and went in, locking it behind him.

Inside, it was dark. He felt around on the wall to either side of the door for a switch, only found one after his eyes had adjusted enough to see it, low on the wall, at knee level.

The room was as simple as Borchert's. A counter and a small kitchen in the back of the room. A single chair, this one with a sort of net webbing draped over it. A bed, in this case, three feet long, flush to the floor, pushed against one wall.

In the bed, a mutilated head rode on the pillow, the rest of the body covered by a blanket. He knelt down beside it. The eyes had been dug out, the lids cut off as well. The ears had been shorn away to leave two whirls of slick pink flesh. The nose, too, was gone, leaving a dark gaping hole. The lips seemed to have been gnawed mostly away, perhaps by the teeth that now loomed through their gap.

As he watched, the flesh on the face shivered and the head turned slightly, the missing eyes seeming to bore into his own eyes. He broke the gaze and then, grabbing the blanket, tugged it off the body.

Underneath was only a torso, all limbs gone, nipples cut away, penis severed. He sat watching the chest rise and fall, air whistling between the teeth. There was something wrong with the way the body lay, he realized, and he pushed it over onto the side a little, enough to see that the buttocks had been shaved away.

The mouth said something urgently but he couldn't understand what because most of the tongue was gone. He let go of the body. He looked away, let himself slip from his knees to lie on the floor. Behind him, he could hear someone pounding at the door. He stayed there, staring up at the ceiling, listening to Aline babble, until they came and dragged him away.

"So," said Borchert, "now you've seen for yourself." He was standing using a cane, precariously grounded in his palm to support himself. Kline was in the chair now, Borchert's chair, having been brought there by the guards after they had dragged him by the feet out of Aline's room and down the stairs, his head bumping against each step.

"What's wrong with you?" asked Borchert. "You look feverish."

"Aline's alive," said Kline.

"Of course he's alive," said Borchert. "I must apologize for lying, Mr. Kline, but trust I had my reasons."

"Why?"

"Why, Mr. Kline?" Borchert turned, moved closer by hopping slightly. "You want to know?"

"Yes."

Borchert smiled. "Knowledge is the most valuable of commodities," he said. "Shall we trade? I'll trade you knowledge for a limb."

"What?"

"You heard me," said Borchert. "Knowledge for a limb. You choose the limb. Or even just a hand or foot. That should be enough."

"No," said Kline.

"That's you're problem," said Borchert. "You don't want to know badly enough."

"I want to know," said Kline.

"Truth or flesh," said Borchert. "Which is more important?"

Kline didn't answer.

"Or say just a digit," said Borchert. "A single finger or toe. What does a finger or toe matter? You've already lost eight digits. What difference would one more make?"

Kline stood up, made for the door. He could hear Borchert behind him, chuckling.

"The offer stands, Mr. Kline," he said. "Come back any time."

He lay in bed, thinking. With the light off he kept seeing Aline's mutilated face, the head riding up on the pillow, blankets tucked just below the chin. Eventually he got up and turned the light on.

His foot ached. It was still weeping blood and fluid where the toes had been, and the foot itself was oddly dark, seemed swollen. He put it on a pillow, kept it elevated, which seemed to help a little.

What was the truth? he wondered. How important was it to know? And once he knew, what then?

He looked at his stump. He could still, sometimes, feel the hand there. And, when Borchert had drugged him, he had been able to see it as well, half-present, like a ghost. He tried to will himself to see it again, could not.

Maybe there was someone who could give him something for his foot, he thought, an anti-inflammatory or perhaps something more, before the foot became too swollen, too painful, to walk on. He would take that, and then stay in bed, waiting for the toes to heal.

Why? he wondered, again seeing Aline's face despite the light still being on. Why had Borchert lied to him? What did he have to gain by pretending Aline was dead when he was actually alive?

He kept turning the question around in his head.

And when, at last, he came up with an answer, he realized he was in very great trouble indeed.

IX.

The guard at the gate didn't want to admit him when he arrived, but Kline told him he was coming for an amputation, that Borchert had invited him to return. The guard consulted his fellow behind the door and then waited with Kline at the gate in the dark while the latter guard went upstairs to consult Borchert.

"It's very late," said the guard.

"He'll see me," said Kline. "He told me to come."

And indeed, when the other guard returned, he was admitted.

He went with the other guard up the stairs to Borchert's room. The guard knocked. When Borchert called back, the guard opened the door and allowed Kline to enter alone.

"Well," said Borchert. "Truth is important to you after all, Mr. Kline."

He was sitting in his chair, a gun in his hand gripped awkwardly with his remaining fingers. "Please stay right there, Mr. Kline," he said.

"It's not loaded," said Kline.

"No?" said Borchert. "What makes you think that?"

"The gun you gave me wasn't," said Kline.

"No, it wasn't," said Borchert, "but wasn't that perhaps because I was giving it to you?"

Kline didn't answer.

"Care to tell me what you know?" asked Borchert.

"You're planning to kill Aline," said Kline.

"And?"

"And planning to make it look like I killed him."

"You've been most obliging in that regard," said Borchert. "You've acted your role nicely. A documented penchant for violence. A certain obsession with Aline, dead or alive. You're only wrong in one particular, that being that I've already killed Aline."

"When?"

"Not long after you last left. For a limbless man he put up quite a fight."

"Why?"

"Ah," said Borchert. "Mr. Kline, I doubt if I can make you understand."

"Try me."

"*Try me*, Mr. Kline? How colloquial of you. It was a matter of belief. Aline and I disagreed on certain particulars, questions of belief. Either he or I had to be done away with for the good of the faith in a way that would leave the survivor blameless. Otherwise there would have been a schism. Naturally, I, in my position, preferred that he be done away with rather than I."

"You were enemies."

"Not at all. Each of us admired the other. It was simply an expedient political move, Mr. Kline. It had to be done."

"Why me?"

"Why you, Mr. Kline? Simply because you were there, and because God had touched you with His grace, had chosen you by removing your hand. You'll of course be rewarded in heaven for your role in all this. Whether you'll be rewarded in this life, though, is entirely another matter."

"Perhaps I should go," said Kline.

"A good question, Mr. Kline. Do I kill you or do I let you go? Hmmm? What do you think, Mr. Kline? Shall I let you go? Shall we flip a coin?"

Kline did not answer.

"No coin?" asked Borchert. "Do you care to express an opinion?"

"I'd like to go," said Kline.

"Of course you would," said Borchert. "And so you shall. Today shall be a day for mercy, not justice. Perhaps, with a little luck, you'll even be able to make it out the gate and past the guards to the so-called freedom of the outside world."

Kline turned toward the door.

"But then again," he heard from behind him, "surely justice must temper mercy, Mr. Kline. Am I right? So perhaps you'd care to leave a little something we can remember you by."

Kline stood still. And then, without turning around, he reached slowly for the door handle.

"I wouldn't do that if I were you," said Borchert. "I hate to shoot a man in the back."

Kline stopped, turned to face him.

"What do you want?" he asked.

"You know exactly what I want," said Borchert, his eye steady. "Flesh for knowledge."

"No," said Kline.

"You told the guard you'd come up here for an amputation," said Borchert. "There's a cleaver on the counter. The same cleaver you used on my finger. Where the hand is gone, the arm shall follow. Otherwise I shoot you. It makes honestly no difference to me, Mr. Kline. You've accomplished your purpose. Technically, you're no longer needed."

Kline started slowly for the back of the room. Borchert watched him go, pushing at the floor with his foot to turn his chair around.

The cleaver was there, imbedded in the butcher's block.

"Go ahead, Mr. Kline. Take it by the cronge and tug it free."

He took the cleaver by the handle. "What's to stop me from killing you?" he asked.

"Do you really know how to throw a cleaver, Mr. Kline? Where does one learn such skills? Some sort of Vocational and Technical school? Can you imagine you'd be able to hit me, let alone hit me so that the blade itself will stick? And even if you did, I imagine I'd be able to squeeze off a shot beforehand—"

"Assuming the gun is loaded."

"Assuming the gun is loaded," agreed Borchert affably. "A shot that would bring the guards running and that would get you killed. So, Mr. Kline, you'd be trading the possibility of killing me for your own life. Is that really what you want to do? No? Now be a good boy and cut off your arm."

◆ ◆ ◆

He turned on the burner in the countertop, waited for it to heat up. The cleaver seemed sharp enough, though he realized it might have some difficulty cutting through bone. If he hit the joint just right it probably wouldn't matter, though he shouldn't forget he was cutting left-handed; did he have sufficient force in his left hand to cut all the way through in a single blow?

He lined the cleaver along the crease of his elbow, found the flesh to run almost from one end of the blade to the other. He would have to hit it exactly right.

In his mind's eye, the cleaver is already coming swiftly down, beginning to bite through skin and flesh and bone. He will be washed over with pain and will stagger, but before going down he must remember to thrust the new end of his arm against the burner to cauterize it, so that he doesn't bleed to death. And then, if he is still standing, he may manage to stagger from the room and down the stairs and eventually out of the compound altogether, where, limping, feverish, in pain, he will make his way out into the lone and dreary world.

And this, he realizes, is only the best possible outcome. In all probability it will be much worse. The hatchet will strike wrong and he will have to strike a second time. He will wooze and fall before cauterizing the wound and then lie on the floor bleeding to death from the wound. The guards will catch him at the gate and kill him. Or even worse, all will go well, the arm coming smoothly off, but Borchert, smiling, will say "Very good, Mr. Kline. But why stop there? What shall we cut off next?"

He raises the cleaver high. His whole life is waiting for him. He only needs to bring the cleaver down for it to begin.

LAST DAYS

You've only got one finger left,
And it's pointing toward the door.
—*Beck, "Lord Only Knows"*

PART ONE

The second time was worse than the first, both because he already knew how it would feel and because of how much thicker an elbow is than a wrist. Still, he managed it, left-handed, despite Borchert's pistol trained at his head. First he carefully tied a tourniquet around the upper arm and then brought the cleaver down hard, chopping all the way through on the first try, and then he thrust the stump against the burner. The stump sizzled and smoked, his vision starting to go. He shook his head and took two steps toward Borchert, and then collapsed.

After that, it became more complicated. He came conscious to find Borchert kneeling beside him, still aiming the pistol, grinning eagerly down.

"And what," Borchert asked, eyes glittering, "shall we cut off next?"

He struck Borchert as hard as he could in the throat and the man fell back, gasping. Kline dragged his way on top of him, managing to get to Borchert's gun in time to jam a thumb into the guard behind its trigger. He bore down with his full weight, working his way slowly up Borchert's body while the latter kept squeezing the gun's trigger, trying to tear off his thumb. A moment later, Kline broke Borchert's nose with his forehead.

It took a few more blows before the man was unconscious and Kline could wrest the gun away. Then he stuffed Borchert's mouth with the sash of his robe. Straddling the man's chest, he slapped him softly until his eyes opened.

I feel fine, *he tried to tell himself while it was going on, though he felt as though he were some distance from his body.* I've never felt better. *His missing arm didn't even hurt. He wondered idly how long it would be before he died of shock.*

"Hello, Borchert," he said, when the man's eyes focused, and then he reached out and strangled him with his single hand. It was hard to get a good grip, and hard to keep hold. At a certain moment, he began to feel dizzy, and was afraid he might pass out. But by the time that moment had passed, Borchert seemed mostly dead.

After that, it became more complicated still.

I.

Light, then dark, then light again. Something pressing into his cheek. Sounds dopplering toward him and away, cars maybe. The taste of blood in his mouth and then his mouth filling with blood and he had to make an effort to cough it up so as to breathe. Slowly his mouth filled with blood again. Almost certainly he was bleeding to death. He kept taking slow breaths and then coughing blood and then taking slower and slower breaths. After a while he stopped hearing anything and it was nothing but dark. He tried to keep breathing anyway.

Once he'd stopped breathing, he opened his eyes. He was in a hospital bed, tubing running from an IV into his arm. He thought he should get up, but when he tried it felt like a knife was being driven hilt-deep into his eye. So he stopped trying.

Instead, he lay there, staring first at the curtain screening the bed off from the rest of the room and then into the bank of fluorescent lights above him. When he closed his eyes, the lights were still there, gathered behind his eyelids, sharp and clear.

Probably really a hospital, he thought, eyes still closed. *Which could be good or bad. But never as bad as if it isn't really a hospital.*

It took him awhile to notice that the rest of his arm was now missing, lopped off at the shoulder joint. Awkwardly, he unwrapped the dressing, peeling the stained gauze away. Whoever had done it had done a professional job, the stump's end smooth and expertly blocked off, evenly cauterized, suppurating just slightly.

When he flexed his shoulder, the absent arm throbbed and the stump seeped a little faster. His missing hand throbbed less, almost not at all. Worst of all was the stretch between wrist and elbow that he had cut off himself as Borchert watched. The missing flesh and bone above that, from elbow to shoulder, removed without his knowledge, just tingled slightly.

He tried to clamber out of bed again, felt again the stabbing pain in his eye. When he tried again, he got a little farther, but then the pain grew so vivid that the room spun completely away.

When he opened his eyes again a man was sitting beside him, wearing a blue smock and staring at a metal clipboard. He was frowning slightly. Kline watched him turn pages, light gathering and spilling from his glasses as his head moved. There was, pinned to his smock, a name plaque: Morand.

"Ah," Morand said, and smiled. "Decided to live, did we, Mr. Kline?"

His smile slowly faded when Kline didn't respond. "No offense," he said.

"None taken," Kline managed. His voice, weak, didn't sound much like his voice.

"You shouldn't have unwrapped that," said Morand, pointing to his shoulder. He came around to squint at it. "Healing nicely, though," he said.

He drew Kline's foot out from under the blanket and removed the sock, then removed the dressing. Three of his toes were missing, Kline noticed, then remembered what had happened to them. "These were quite a mess," Morand said. "You're lucky not to lose the foot."

He wrote something on the clipboard.

"I have a few questions for you," Morand said. "First, how do you feel about what's happened to you?"

"What exactly did happen?"

"Your arm," said Morand. "It's not easy to lose such a large part of you. How do you feel, scale of one to ten?"

LAST DAYS • 103

Kline looked at the back of the clipboard. "Is ten good or bad?" he asked.

"Seven or eight is *good*. That makes ten somewhere along the lines of *superlative* or *never been better*, depending on how effusive you are."

"I was already missing a hand," said Kline. "I was mostly used to that."

"Shall we call you a four then?" asked Morand. "Am I reading you correctly? I'm sorry we had to take the rest of the arm," he said, and leaned toward Kline's stump. "Though it came out nicely, if I do say so myself. Sit up, please."

"I can't," said Kline.

"Why not?"

"When I raise my head, it feels like I'm being stabbed in the eye."

"I see," said Morand, and smiled. "Probably due to your having been shot in the head."

"Shot in the head?"

Morand's smile faded again. "You don't remember?" He took from his pocket a round mirror about the size of an eyeball, affixed to a pen-like metal stylus, and held it out. "You've already seen the worst," he said.

Kline took it awkwardly. "Isn't this a dentist's mirror?" he asked. "For mouths?"

"Technically, yes," said the doctor.

"I thought doctors wore their mirrors on their heads. For light or something."

"Not this doctor," Morand said.

Kline spun the stylus about with his fingers until he saw part of his face in the mirror, the reflection shivering slightly. His head, he saw when he turned the mirror minutely, was heavily bandaged. He watched Morand slowly unwind it, working down to a thick pad of gauze, dark with blood and flux.

When Kline reached up to touch it, Morand stopped him.

"We'll change the dressing in a moment," Morand said. "You can look then."

"Where am I?" Kline asked.

"Hospital bed," said Morand, surprised. "I thought that would be obvious. You seemed like you were doing all right, considering."

"In a hospital?"

"Naturally. Where else would a hospital bed be?"

"Am I free to leave?"

"We're hardly in a condition to leave, are we?" said Morand, and smiled. "By we, I mean you. Frankly it's a little surprising you're alive at all. For a while you were dead, technically speaking. Were you aware of that? Of course, *technically dead* is nothing compared to *dead*."

"Is that a threat?"

The doctor looked surprised again. "What have I said to offend you?"

"Will you open the curtain?"

"The curtain?" asked Morand. "Why?"

"I just want to see for myself what's on the other side."

"But I've already told you, this is a hospital."

"Please," said Kline, "open the curtain."

Morand looked at him a moment and then shrugged and turned away. As Kline hid the dentist's mirror under his blanket, Morand pulled the curtain back: three other beds, a door leading out into a bright hall. *Just a hospital*, Kline thought, and began to relax. *Nothing to worry about at all.*

A nurse came in and began to peel the gauze away from the side of his head, carefully. Morand groped absently in his vest pocket, then checked his other pockets, then searched the bedside table and the blanket with his eyes.

"What is it?" Kline asked.

"Can't seem to find my mirror," said Morand.

"Dentist's mirror? I haven't seen it," Kline claimed.

Morand groped through his pockets again then shrugged and went out. He returned a moment later with a larger mirror, this one affixed to a stiff but flexible cable, a clamp at the cable's end. He clamped it onto Kline's IV stand, then positioned the stand beside the bed, adjusting the mirror until Kline saw himself in it.

The dressing was off now. The nurse dabbed at the wound with a moist pad, slowly breaking the crust away. The wound was big and jagged, a crazed network of stitches running all along one side of his head.

"We got out the bullet, what didn't come out on its own," said the doctor. "Most of it anyway."

The nurse kept dabbing, leaning against the edge of the bed. Kline watched her in the mirror, listened to the sound of her breathing.

"Your biggest worry," said Morand, "is the brain. Also internal bleeding. I'd give up jogging for a while if I were you."

The nurse gave a high, tittering laugh.

"The pain in your eye is worrisome. We can put a shunt in, if it's a brain issue," said Morand. "For now, shall we just watch you?"

The nurse covered the wound again with gauze, beginning to rewrap his head.

"We'll just keep an eye on you," Morand said absently.

"What?" said Kline, suddenly nervous.

"What?" said the doctor. His smile came back. "Nothing to worry about, Mr. Kline," he said. "It's for your own good."

They drew the curtains back around the bed as they left, but he didn't hear the door close. He lay staring up at the lights, listening to the echoes of their footsteps down the hall, the alternation between the doctor's treble voice and the nurse's high laugh.

After a while, the telephone began to ring. It was on the bedside table just beside him, on the same side as his missing arm. To reach it, he would have had to roll onto his stump and stretch. He couldn't imagine how that would feel.

So he didn't reach. Instead, he just listened. It rang six times and then stopped. And then rang six more times, and then stopped. And then rang six more times. After that it didn't ring again.

Six-six-six, he thought. *Mark of the beast*. And then thought, *They know exactly where I am*.

It made him restless. He made himself sit up again, this time slower and with more care. It still felt like someone was pushing a knife into his eye, but slower now. And once he was seated, the pain slowly faded to a dull ache.

The phone was still on the wrong side, silent now. On this side was the curtain. He stretched his arm out as far as he could, but still couldn't reach it. When he started to twist toward it, the pain in his eye gathered, then spread.

He tried to extend his reach with the dentist's mirror, was still short. He pulled the mirror clamped to the IV stand closer, straightening its cable as far as it would go, then twisted the stand's pole with his wrist until the mirror touched the curtain.

He twisted the pole further and the mirror brushed its way past, ruffling the curtain. He twisted the mirror back toward him, cocked the end of the cable slightly, then twisted the pole back out until the mirror was touching the curtain again. Then he spun the pole hard.

The movement sent a wave of pain through the remnants of his shoulder and deep into the abyss of his eye. He closed both eyes and bit down on the insides of his mouth and squinted hard. It seemed to help.

When he opened his eyes again, he could taste blood in his mouth. The curtain had slid three inches or so along its track, leaving a slight gap near the wall, just behind his head.

He tried again and more than doubled the gap, then once more, which left the curtain open enough, but not so much to look like it hadn't simply been carelessly closed. It was harder to work the IV stand and its mirror into place without passing out, but in the end he had positioned them near the edge of the curtain, mirror pressed against the wall. If he held the dentist's mirror just right, he could look into the larger mirror and have an unimpeded view of the doorway.

A few hours passed before anyone came through the door. When someone did, it was just one man, large of frame, balding, who still had all his limbs. He came in and stopped, then came near the curtain.

Kline hid the dentist's mirror under the sheet, watched the tips of the man's shoes just beneath the curtain.

"Mr. Kline?" the man said.

Kline didn't respond. He watched through veiled eyes as the man slowly dragged back the curtain and then came to stand beside the bed. He was motionless and silent for a moment, and then his footsteps echoed off across the room. When they returned, he was carrying a chair.

He sat down beside the bed, crossing his arms.

Just past him, another flicker passed through the doorway and disappeared. A moment later, it slipped back into Kline's limited vision to become human, a uniformed police officer.

The officer put his hand on the first man's shoulder.

"Asleep is he, Frank?" the officer asked.

"I'll wake him up soon," Frank said.

"Where do you want me, buddy?"

Frank shrugged. "Doesn't matter. In here, if you want. Or just outside the door."

The police officer went and got another chair, carried it over to a corner, sat down. Almost immediately he was sprawled in it. Shortly thereafter was asleep.

After a while Frank reached out, nudged Kline slightly. "You're not asleep," he said. "I can tell."

"Never claimed to be," said Kline.

Frank smirked. "Shifty, are we?" he said. "Kline is it?"

"That's right," said Kline.

"Used to be a cop?"

Kline nodded.

"Undercover," said Frank. "That's no cop. It's someone doesn't know who he is. You know who you are, Kline?"

"Better than you," said Kline.

"Don't be too sure," said Frank. Reaching into one pocket, he pulled out a folded piece of paper. He carefully unfolded it and smoothed the creases out.

"Says here," he said, "*missing a hand*. I'd say that's an understatement, wouldn't you, Kline? How'd you lose your hand?"

"I let someone cut it off," said Kline.

"Now why would a man go and do a thing like that?"

"You can read about it in the papers."

"I don't suppose you care to tell me how you lost the rest of the arm? And the toes?"

"Long story."

"I've got time," Frank said. He waited. When Kline didn't say anything, he stretched. "Bunch of mutilates south of here," he said.

"That right?" said Kline.

Frank nodded. "A whole compound's worth. The Holy Christian Fellowship of Amputation or some such thing," he said. "The Brotherhood of Mutilation. They been asking after you."

Kline didn't say anything.

"You know why they're asking?" asked Frank.

"Why?"

"They don't care to say. They just seem to want to get in touch with you."

"They've already found me," said Kline.

"They pay you a social call?"

"Not yet," said Kline.

Frank got up and walked slowly around the bed. "You want me to put my cards on the table?" he asked.

"I wasn't aware we were playing cards," said Kline.

"Not much you do know, apparently." Frank scratched his head, turning to look at the curtain. "The way I see it is this: a few weeks back you show up on the side of a country road, delirious, mostly dead. Some good Samaritan catches a glimpse of you sprawled on the shoulder and calls 911. I go out there and what I see is lots of blood and an arm cut back to the elbow, recently and awkwardly done. I'm thinking I got a corpse but you turn out to still be breathing. Shallow breaths: slowly suffocating to death. So out of the goodness of my heart I get you to a hospital. With me so far?"

Kline nodded.

"Same day, earlier on, I get a call from somebody about a fire in the middle of nowhere. I send an officer out and he comes back telling me it's this cult compound. One of the buildings has caught fire. 'Anybody hurt or dead?' I ask him. 'Don't know,' he says, 'they wouldn't let me in.'"

Frank turned to Kline.

"He's just a young kid," he said. "Didn't know any better. Would have been me, I sure as hell would have gotten in. But by the time I get down there myself, the fire's out and it's all cleaned up, no sign of much amiss. They stop me at the gate, explain it's all taken care of. Each of those guards only has one hand, a kind of gun prosthesis where the other one used to be. Is that legal? Probably not, but what do I know? What I do know is I can get in, but if I do somebody's likely to get hurt. And it's too late for me to find out anything they don't want me to find out. So I let it go."

Frank sat back down again.

"And then you show up. Any time you find two one-legged men at the same dance it's no coincidence." He leaned toward Kline. "Got anything to say yet?"

"Not yet," said Kline.

"I got time," said Frank. "I'm in no rush. I'll give you a few hours to think it through." He pointed to the officer in the chair. "Davis here will keep you honest, even though the doctor says you wouldn't get far. Doesn't pay to underestimate a man who can bring himself to chop off his own hand to buy himself a few minutes to think." He smiled grimly. "Maybe I do know a little about you after all."

He stood and rubbed his hand along the back of his neck, as if smoothing his collar down.

"So, care to tell me what you were doing there?"

"Doing where?"

"You know where," Frank said, and made a disgusted face. "Mine's not a pretty job to start with," he said. "Someone like you should know better."

Kline didn't say anything. His eye felt like it was being stabbed, but softer now, with a butter knife. Either the pain was lessening or he was getting used to it. Maybe both. He squeezed the eye shut and waited for the pain to pass.

"How did you lose the arm?" asked Frank.

"Who shot you in the head?" Frank asked.

"Why are the mutilates looking for you?" asked Frank.

"Don't want to answer now?" said Frank. "Fine. I'm off to have dinner and see the girlfriend. I'll be back early tomorrow. You'll answer when I come back, I guarantee."

The pain was suddenly gone. He opened the eye. Davis, he saw, was awake now, alert.

"You a cult member?" Frank asked on his way out the door. "A mutilate?"

"No," Kline said.

"There's at least that," said Frank, and went out.

◆◆◆

Davis sat in the chair, slightly slumped, arms crossed, feet out in front of him and crossed at the ankles, staring at Kline.

"How long you been on the force?" Kline finally asked.

"None of your goddamn business," said Davis.

"What's the matter?" asked Kline, surprised. "I'm just making conversation."

"You think you have Frank fooled," said Davis. "But you're not pulling the wool over my eyes. And you're wrong about Frank, too."

"What wool?" asked Kline. "I don't even know what you're talking about."

"That's it," said Davis. "I've had enough of you."

Kline watched him pick up the chair and carry it out into the hall. He put it to one side of the doorframe and sat down. All Kline could see of him was, cutting into the doorway slightly, a sliver of his shoulder and his arm.

III.

He was walking toward a guard with a gun in the place of a hand. The guard lifted his arm and tensed his forearm slightly and the gun rattled oddly and then fired. He felt his head jerked around and found himself lying on the ground, dirt and blood filling his mouth. There was a strangeness to everything, as if the separation between things and himself was much less distinct than he had previously supposed, as if he was blurring into the world around him. He had, he realized, a gun in his own hand, but not in place of a hand. He was lying on it, it was somewhere beneath his ribs. Could he move? No. If he aimed at the guard through his own chest and squeezed the trigger would he be able to kill the guard before the guard shot him again?

The guard was coming toward him, footsteps heavy and slow. There was something odd about his footsteps, a kind of chiming to them, metal on metal. And they seemed to last longer than footsteps should. He made a tremendous effort to roll over enough to get the gun out from under him, and felt as if a knife was being stabbed into his eye. But it was enough: the gun was out and in front of him and he was squeezing the trigger.

"What's that?" a nurse was saying to him, a new nurse, nobody he remembered seeing before. Her features were softened by the darkness. "It looks like a dentist's mirror."

He just watched her, still brandishing the dentist's mirror. Next to her, on the bedside table, the telephone was ringing.

"If you're here to see the dentist you're in the wrong place," she said, uncradling the telephone. "Hello?" she said.

The knife slid slowly out of his eye and back into God's sheath. He slipped the dentist's mirror beneath the blanket.

"He's right here," she said. "May I ask who's calling?"

He watched her nod, then hold the receiver away from her mouth, muffling it with her palm.

"Your wife," she said.

"I don't have a wife," he said.

"You don't?" she said, and looked thoughtful. "To be honest, from the voice I was surprised it was even a woman."

"Give me the phone," he said. "I think I know who it is."

It was awkward settling the receiver against the wrong side of his face with the wrong hand. *But why?* he wondered. *I've been missing the other hand long enough that I should be used to this.* But losing the rest of his arm seemed to have changed something inside his head, to have transformed him somehow.

"Hello," he said.

"Mr. Kline?" a voice said. It was flat, grainy, with something seriously wrong with it. But vaguely familiar as well.

"Speaking," he said. "Who is this?"

"You know who this is. You've caused a lot of trouble," the voice said.

"I didn't ask for any of it. And I don't know who this is."

"Who asks for anything? That's not how life works."

"Who is it?" the nurse beside him was asking. "Is it a prank call?"

"Mr. Kline," said the voice.

"What?" said Kline.

"What's going on?" he heard Davis say, waking up. *Some guard*, Kline thought. Davis was standing now, a dark shape framed in the light of the open doorway. Then he turned the light on and stood there blinking, his face puffy.

"Nothing," said Kline to him.

"Mr. Kline," said the voice, "we're coming for you." And then the line went dead.

◆ ◆ ◆

He told the nurse the call had been a prank, nothing to worry about, just a friend trying to be funny. "Some friend," she suggested. She and Davis wandered unruddered around his room for a while, Davis threatening to call Frank if Kline didn't tell him what the caller had said. The nurse, despite Kline's protests, administered an injection and then left. Davis stayed near the bed watching him suspiciously for a little while, then went back to his seat just outside the door.

Kline lay there wondering how they would kill him. He could feel whatever it was the nurse had given him now starting to work, insects beginning to rustle just beneath his skin. *Surely not here, surely not the hospital,* he thought. Even if they did come, there was Davis there, at the door; he'd hear something.

If he was awake.

I should stay awake, he thought, *I have to*, he thought, even as he felt the dark congeal around him, his face growing numb as glass.

IV.

Later, he came blurrily conscious to a sound he couldn't place, not sure if he had actually heard it or had merely dreamt it. A low burbling. The lights in the room were out now except for a dim glow near the bathroom and a rectangle of light from the hall. What was it he'd heard? The sound wasn't exactly recognizable or familiar; probably the sound, whatever it was, had awoken him.

Something had changed. The hallway struck him as wrong. He stared at the box of light that was the doorway. It was just a doorway, but it still looked wrong. *What am I not seeing?* he wondered. He kept staring, but there was nothing extraordinary about it: it was just a simple doorway.

And then he realized that, yes, that was exactly what was extraordinary about it: where were Davis' shoulder and arm?

Nothing to worry about, he told himself. *He's just gotten up to use the bathroom. He's moved his chair slightly. That's all.*

But there was still the question of the sound. What had he heard?

He was still mulling it over when a nurse came through the doorway, tugging her scrubs straight. It was not the same nurse as earlier. Perhaps this was the night nurse. But hadn't the last nurse been the night nurse?

Through his lidded eyes, he watched her come. Her shoes were tracking in something, he realized, and then realized with a shock that it was blood.

He watched her come, still pretending to be asleep. He gripped the dentist's mirror tightly, thumbing the stylus' end. It wasn't sharp, though it tapered a little at the tip.

When she was closer, it became obvious one hand was prosthetic. The way she was walking made him think something was wrong with her leg as well: either a serious injury or that leg was artificial as well.

Once she reached his bed, she just stood looking down at him. He watched her take from the pocket of her smock a hypodermic needle encased in a gray plastic sheath. Awkwardly she clicked it onto a syringe. She gave a little twist and the plastic sheath came free to reveal a needle. From the other pocket, she removed a squat plastic vial. Resting it on the bedside table she stuck the needle's end through the lid and drew a liquid, bubbling, up into the syringe.

Inverting the syringe, she tapped the air out.

Now, he thought, tensing slightly, *she will bring the needle close so as to inject it into my arm. When she does, I'll plunge the mirror's stylus into her eye and will kill her dead.*

Only it didn't work quite the way he imagined. Instead of coming close and injecting it into his arm, she simply injected it into his IV bag.

She stood above him, watching, still a little too distant. In the dark, he could see a faint gleam from some part of her face, either her teeth or her eyes.

Slowly, trying to keep the sheets from moving, he turned his hand palm down. He could feel the catheter tug between the bones on the back of his hand, but, taped down, it didn't come free. He flexed his hand first back then forward, trying to catch the thin tubing between his fingers. His mouth was going dry. The tubing was taped too far back on the wrist. There was nothing loose to grab hold of, nothing easy to reach one-handed. He could get to it, but not without her knowing he was awake.

He moved the dentist's mirror out of his fist and held it like a pen, the mirror near his fingertips, the stylus and its tapered tip extending back over the web of his thumb. He bent his wrist back but couldn't catch the IV tubing on the stylus.

Rolling the mirror over between his index and middle finger he tried again, straightening his fingers until the tapered tip touched the back of his wrist. Pushing the mirror down against the mattress, he slid his hand forward. The end of the stylus touched the strip of tape and slipped back over it.

He tried again, slower this time. His tongue had started to feel thick and stiff in his mouth, like the handle of a whip. The stylus touched the tape and caught against its edge a moment and then slipped over.

The third time he got the tip firmly under the tape. He worked it minutely back and forth until he was sure the tape was loose enough and then, using his knuckles as a fulcrum, pulled the tape slowly loose.

It made a slight sound coming off the skin, but the woman didn't notice. The tape came up with the stylus and with it came the catheter, stinging as it pulled out of his vein. He groped for the tubing and held it between his fingers a moment, its wick wet, and then pinched it closed.

She stood beside him, her gaze moving from the IV bag down to him and back again. After a while, she looked at her watch. His mouth was starting to feel like his mouth again, or like somebody's mouth anyway, tingling slightly.

After a while, she picked up the telephone and dialed. He heard her curse and reset the line, then dial again.

He could hear the sound of the ringing between her ear and the telephone. Then he heard a click, a low mumble on the other end of the wire.

"It's me," she said. "Yes," she said, and then waited. "Somebody was outside," she said, and then said, "dead."

"No," she said, "the man outside the door. Two nurses as well.

"No way around it," she said.

"Well, it's done now, no changing it. I had to decide for myself."

He watched her cup the receiver against her shoulder and reach out. He felt her fingers against his hairline, her thumb just below his eyelid, tugging the lid up. He rolled his eye back into his head, then let it float.

"Looks like it," she said. "Hard to be sure in the dark."

"Of course I'll be sure," she said, and let go of his eyelid.

He let his eye slip down until he could see out again through his eyelids. She had turned away now, was facing the IV bag.

"Where?" she was saying. "Just wheel him out like a corpse, then?"

"Yes," she said. "Just as you say."

She reached up and prodded the IV bag with a finger, then pulled the finger back slightly. He watched her stand there, finger outstretched, and waited for her hand to fall. Instead, she prodded the bag again, slower this time.

"Just a minute," she said.

He heard a low rustling on the other end of the line.

"The IV bag," she said. "It's fuller than it should be."

He thought briefly about releasing the cut end of the tubing, letting it drip into the bed. Instead, he groped for the dentist's mirror.

"Probably just a kink in the line," she said. "Hold on."

She turned back toward him, resting the telephone receiver on the bedside table. He could still hear a voice coming out of it. *Be careful*, it was saying. In the half-light she followed the tubing down from the bag, running her fingers along it until she got to the edge of the bed. With one hand, she lowered the railing. She had already pulled the blanket aside, her head down and close to him, before he realized this was finally his chance and drove the end of the stylus as hard as he could up and into her face, the pain in his eye rising immediately to such a pitch that he passed out.

He came conscious to find himself struggling for breath. The woman had fallen onto him, was lying with her shoulder pressed against his mouth. The tubing had come out of his hand and started dripping: the bed was wet on one side. It was wet around his face too, on the pillow, but warmer, and when he turned his head to try to breathe he could see the fluid was dark and from the smell guessed it must be blood.

His shoulder was beginning to throb. He wriggled a little and her shoulder slid off his face, and her neck and ear slid down to replace it. He wriggled again, and pushed with his remaining arm. The head slowly tilted, the ear rolling down his cheekbone and the skull pushing against his face through hair that swept it wetly along and past his lips. The head yawed up and in the darkness he caught the brief glint of the mirror's stylus and then the mirror itself, anchored somewhere in her face, then the rest of the body slipped off the bed and collapsed onto the floor.

He lay there, panting. Hair was caught in his lips and he tried blowing it out and then brushing it away with his hand. He lay still, catching his breath, the pillow's dampness growing tacky, sticky.

Relax, he told himself. *Stay calm.*

But lying there in the dark he kept thinking he could hear her somewhere below him, feebly moving. There was a sound like whispering or something rustling over paper. In the dark below, he couldn't help but imagine her fingers moving, her body slowly gathering itself.

Soon he came to feel it was worse lying there imagining her coming back to life than whatever getting out of bed would do to his eye. Slowly, he swung his legs off the bed and raised his body, his head throbbing. At first, he didn't realize he was standing on her body and then he almost fell trying to figure out how to step off her without slipping or falling. But then almost without knowing it he was out of bed, still conscious, steadying himself against the mattress with one hand.

Still hearing the scuttling, he straightened enough to grope for a light switch, almost falling in reaching for it.

The lights flickered a moment before coming on, sickly white. It hurt his head to look down. When he did, she was there, contorted and face down, head suspended a few inches off the floor by the dentist's mirror, face hidden by the back of her head, a swath of blood along the bed and floor to mark how she had slid. She wasn't moving at all.

It took him a moment of standing and staring to realize that the scuttling was not coming from her but from the table, from the uncradled telephone receiver. He reached out and picked it up, held it against his face.

The scuttling became a whisper, then a voice talking into his ear. *Mlinko*, it was saying. *Tell us what happened, Mlinko. Mlinko, please pick up the telephone.*

He listened for a while, finally said, "This isn't Mlinko."

The whispering stopped. For a moment, he thought the line had gone dead.

When the voice came back, it was no longer a whisper, but still flat, uninflected.

"Mr. Kline," the voice said.

"Yes," said Kline.

"Would you mind putting Mlinko on?"

"Mlinko seems to be dead," said Kline.

"Appears or is?"

"Both," said Kline.

"You've caused a lot of trouble," the voice said.

"I didn't ask for any of it," he could not stop himself from saying.

"Yes," said the voice. "In that case, you must remember how the rest of the conversation goes. We're still coming for you."

V.

Later, once he made it to the loading dock, he wasn't quite sure how he had managed. Only the first part was clear. He had dropped the receiver and then tried to bend down to search Mlinko's pockets, but before he was even bending his knees, he realized that there'd be no getting up again.

He looked for something on the bedside table to use as a weapon, but there was nothing. He pushed off the bed and made slowly for the door. The pain in his eye was still there, more a constant pressure than a lacerating pain as long as he made no quick movements with his shoulder.

He shuffled toward the doorway, feeling as if he were moving underwater. Once there, he balanced against the posts and then moved through the slick of blood. Davis was lying to one side, face up, throat slit, neck cricked back. Two of his fingers had been severed and removed. The blood felt warm through Kline's socks.

He slipped and almost went down, then nearly blacked out and started to go down again. He came to himself clinging to the desk of the nurses' station, on the other side of which were a pair of nurses, both with their throats cut, hands hidden so he couldn't tell if any of their fingers had been freshly amputated. One was the nurse who had answered the telephone earlier. The other he didn't recognize.

He pushed off and started down the hall, his breath coming out in throbs, his shoulder pulsing. The knife was back in his eye, sharp and long. Things began to come in bursts. Suddenly, he was farther down the hall than he thought and he could see a door at the hall's terminus, and without opening it he was on the other side. A scattering of faces reared up around him, frozen and static, like cutouts, stricken with odd expressions, falling quickly away. Another stretch of hall, a slowly descending ramp, then a tight staircase that he tumbled down as much as walked down. Somehow he was still standing when he reached the bottom. Another stretch of hall, this one dimly lit, a series of broken beds lined along one wall, followed by a series of sealed blue plastic bins. Then a double set of swinging doors. By the time things started happening in sequence again, he was slumped over a railing, staring down at the sewer grate below, on some sort of loading dock. *Now what?* he wondered. The dock was empty, no vehicles to be seen. If he followed the railing in one direction, there was a set of stairs he could go down. He could take them down and then climb the incline of the drive out of the hospital. It wasn't too steep, but he still wasn't sure he could make it. In the other direction, the railing ended just before a large green dumpster. There might be a gap between the dumpster and the far wall. Perhaps he could squeeze in.

He was still trying to decide what to do when he realized two figures had started down the drive and were coming quickly, shadows reeling in closer behind them with each step.

He turned and shuffled toward the dumpster. He could hear the dull echo of their footsteps now. *I've been seen,* he thought, but kept moving anyway, slower and slower it felt. He could see the gap better as he came closer, but still wasn't sure if it was big enough.

When he reached it, he saw that it wasn't.

He backed into it as far as he could and waited. It was a little darker there, but not dark enough to hide him. He'd probably been seen. *Or maybe,* he told himself, *they aren't looking for me.*

They came up the loading dock stairs and right to him.

"You're Kline," one of them said, the dark-haired one. He was missing an eye and most of the fingers on one hand. The other hand had been replaced by a gun prosthetic. An ear was gone as well. The other man, blond, lagging slightly behind, seemed only to be missing a hand, his right. His other hand held a gun.

Kline nodded. The inside of his head felt bruised.

"What did you do to Mlinko?" the dark-haired man asked.

"You mean specifically?"

"I mean where is she?"

"She's not anywhere," said Kline. "She's dead."

The man lifted his gun-arm, pointed it at Kline's head. "I suppose you know we've come to kill you," he said.

"I can't say I'm surprised," said Kline.

"Any last words?" asked the blond man, lifting his gun as well.

"I don't know," said Kline.

"You don't know?" said the dark-haired man, raising his eyebrows.

The blond man, Kline realized abruptly, had taken a step back and was now well behind the dark-haired one. He was no longer pointing his gun at Kline: it seemed to be slowly drifting away. A moment more and it was aimed at the dark-haired man's head, just behind his range of vision.

"Yes," said Kline quickly. "I do have something to say."

"What is it?" said the dark-haired man.

Kline opened his mouth but didn't speak, just kept looking from one man to the other, waiting for whatever would happen next.

"Too late," said the dark-haired man. "Time to die," he said, and then he was shot in the head by the blond man. He fell, gargling and frothing until the blond man pushed the snout of his pistol against his ear and shot him again.

The blond man kicked the body once and then put his pistol away. "He cometh not with an olive branch but with a sword. He smiteth," he said, then moved toward Kline, smiling.

"Mr. Kline," he said, holding out his hand. "What a pleasure it is to finally meet you."

PART TWO

PART TWO

He could hear the sound of cars ahead, at some distance—or perhaps only something that sounded like cars. Perhaps only the wind. It was hard to know what he was hearing and what he only hoped to hear. He limped toward the sound.

There was a brief rise and then a dip and then another rise. Something was scraping the lining of his skull. He came out of the scrub and went down into the dip and stopped in a sickly stand of cottonwood edging a dried streambed. After that, there was no cover, only sparse dry grasses and dirt.

He leaned against the tree awhile. Yes, he thought, almost certainly cars. He tried to imagine climbing the rise and seeing asphalt at the top, but he couldn't imagine it. Before he knew it, his body had slipped and he was sitting, stump throbbing. He wasn't sure he'd be able to stand up again, let alone make it up the rise.

With his remaining hand, he unwrapped his stump. Its extreme showed the dead circles from the burner, pus seeping through where he had burnt it too deeply, two lumps just below the elbow that must have been the sheared bones. He covered it up again.

The blood in his shoe had grown sticky, the outside of the shoe pasty with dust and blood. He could tell from the blood dripping down his face and onto his shoulder that his head was bleeding, but he was afraid to touch it. The only time he'd touched it, his fingers had gone in deeper than he'd thought possible.

He sat leaning against the tree, trying not to lie down. His hands felt like they were curling in on themselves and dying, even the hand that wasn't there.

After a while he managed to move his hand enough to fumble a sharp stone off the ground. He prodded the end of his stump with it. It made it feel like a knife was being pushed into his eye, but he felt almost alive again too. Yawing and drunken, he crashed up to his feet, lungs feeling like they were drawing in something other than air. He took a step and saw the ground flash toward him and then flash away, and then he was walking somehow, his vision such that he could only just distinguish between earth and sky. What had sounded like cars now sounded like rock scraping against rock, the pain slowly fading back to the same dull, shocked ache he had felt for hours now.

Gradually he made out the shape of the rise. He moved toward it and slowly started up. The sound warped, became more like cars again. He watched the ground in front of him and tried to lean toward it enough to keep moving forward, but not so far as to fall.

About halfway up, he thought he was going to fall backward and had to tack to one side. His feet kept trying to turn downslope; it was all he could do to keep crabbing uphill. His body felt like a separate animal. He could only watch it, encourage it on.

And then dust and scrub grass vanished, replaced by ash-gray gravel and, just beyond that, the asphalt of a two-lane road. Not a car to be seen in either direction. He took a step onto the gravel and then another step, and then collapsed.

I.

When he awoke, he was screaming. He was not on a roadside, he was not on a hospital loading dock; he was in a bed, but not in the bed he had been in before, not the bed he had expected to be in.

"You're awake, then," said a blond man beside him who was missing his right hand.

It was a hospital bed, Kline saw, but he wasn't in a hospital. Instead, he appeared to be in a sort of old-fashioned drawing room: thick brocaded drapes, a grand piano, herringbone parquet floors.

On the wall directly across from him were two paintings which, despite gilt frames, seemed remarkably out of place. One was a simple portrait of a man's head, except the face had been gouged out to leave a pink, cone-shaped hole. The other, all grays and browns, showed a man wearing a leather helmet, leg amputated to the middle of his thigh. One arm was mostly missing, the other arm either partly missing or wrapped up and invisible. He was either blind or his eyes had rolled back into his head. He was either singing or screaming, Kline couldn't say which. Beside him lay a woman partly swallowed by a cloth bag, lying in a puddle of blood.

The blond man, he realized, was observing him closely, almost hungrily. Kline turned his head slightly to meet his gaze. The man didn't blink.

"Which do you prefer?" the man asked with a slight smile, gesturing at the paintings behind him.

"Does it matter?" asked Kline.

The man's face fell. "Of course it matters," he said.

"Is this a test?"

"Why would it be a test? It's just a simple question of taste."

"What if I say I like them both?"

"Do you like them both? Exactly the same?"

"What am I doing here exactly?" asked Kline. "What's all this about?"

"Where are my manners?" said the man. He reached out as if to lay his hand on Kline's remaining arm, instead touched Kline lightly with his stump. "You're with us," he said confidentially. "Trust me, you're safe here," he said.

"Who are you?"

"Call me Paul," said the man.

"Are you planning to kill me, Paul?"

"What a strange idea," said Paul.

"How long have I been here?"

Paul shrugged. "A few days," he said.

"Where's here?" asked Kline.

Paul smiled. "No need to worry about that now," he said.

"But," said Kline.

"No buts," said Paul, standing up now and moving toward the door. "You're still far from well. Lie back now. Try to sleep."

But he couldn't sleep. He lay in the bed, staring at the two paintings, the one on the left precise and clinical, the one on the right chiaroscuro and looking as though it had been done while the artist was channeling an insane Dutch master. The light coming through the window's panes slowly shifted, shuffling about the walls and then disappearing. The windows went slowly dark and opaque, the room lit by a single lamp to one side of him, near the wingchair in which Paul had been sitting. It was harder now to make the paintings out, the light from the lamp catching in the paint and beryling there, hiding the image behind.

In the half-light he began to grow anxious. He sat up slowly. His head ached but not as much as it had in the hospital. When he moved his shoulder, he still felt pressure in his eye, but nothing more. His legs were sore and worked only reluctantly, but after a moment he had edged his legs out of the bed and was standing.

Almost immediately, a blond man was beside him, touching his elbow lightly. He was not sure where the man had come from, certainly not through the door. From behind one of the curtains perhaps?

"You should rest," the blond man was saying in a soothing voice. "There's no need to get up." It was not the same man he had seen before, he realized, not Paul, although they looked similar. This man had a thicker face, was shorter.

"What do you want?" asked Kline.

"Is there something you need?" asked the man. "If you tell me what you need, I'll do my best to retrieve it for you."

"Where's Paul?" he asked.

"I'm Paul," the man said.

"Paul was the other one," said Kline. "You're not Paul."

"We're all Paul," the man said. He touched Kline lightly on the chest, nudged him until he sat on the bed. "Please," he said. "Please rest."

He let the second Paul coax him fully back into the bed, lifting up one of his legs and then the other, then dragging them over until he was lying again where he had been, in the half-light, staring at the vague shapes of the paintings. The Paul circled around behind his head and disappeared.

Getting out of the bed, even briefly, seemed to have exhausted him. Perhaps Paul, the second Paul, had been right.

In the morning he was awoken by a third blond man also missing his right hand. He came in through the door, a tray balanced precariously on his stump. He settled the tray on the bedside table, helped Kline to sit up, then moved the tray onto Kline's lap. Little silver vessels nestled fruits and a hardboiled egg and thick slices of bacon. There were toast points in each corner of the tray like a garnish and a glass of milk and a glass of orange juice.

Kline reached out and took the egg. He took a bite out of it, then looked into the chalky, cooked yolk. The blond man murmured approval.

"What is it?" asked Kline. Looking at him more closely, he could see that his hair wasn't naturally blond. It had been dyed.

"I was certain you'd take the egg first," said the man.

"You were?"

The man nodded, smiled.

"Is everything a test here?"

The man's smile fell. "I didn't mean to offend you," he said. "I would never presume to test you, friend Kline."

Kline grunted, put the rest of the egg in his mouth and chewed.

"What's your name?" Kline asked.

"I'm Paul," said the man.

"You're not," said Kline.

"We all are," he said.

Kline shook his head. "You can't all be Paul," he said.

"Why not?" said the man. "Is this a teaching?"

"A teaching?" said Kline. "What's that supposed to mean?"

"Should I write it down?"

"Write what down?"

"'You can't all be Paul.' And whatever else comes thereafter from your lips."

"No," said Kline, a strange dread starting to grow within him. "I don't want you to write anything down."

"Is that too a teaching?" said Paul. "'Write nothing down'?"

"Nothing's a teaching," said Kline. "Stop saying that."

Kline started into the bacon. As he ate, Paul stared at him, his brow creased in concentration, as if afraid to miss something.

"Am I a prisoner here?" Kline asked.

"A prisoner?" said Paul. "But we're helping you."

"I want to leave," said Kline.

"Why?" asked Paul. "We believe in you, friend Kline," he said. "Why would you want to leave? You're not healed yet."

"You haven't always been called Paul, have you?" Kline said.

Paul looked surprised. "No," he admitted reluctantly.

"What did you used to be called?"

"I'm not allowed to say," said Paul. "It's a dead name. 'You must lose yourself to find yourself.' That's a teaching."

"It's all right to say," said Kline. "You can tell me." Paul looked to either side of him and then leaned forward, whispering into Kline's ear: "Brian."

"Brian?" said Kline.

Paul winced.

"Why Paul?" asked Kline. "Why are you all Paul?"

"Because of the Apostle," said Paul. "And the other one, the philosopher's brother."

"What's this all about?"

"A work," said Paul, his cadence slightly odd as if he were a child reciting something memorized. "A marvelous work and a wonder, such as has never come to pass before in the world of men." He leaned in closer. "We have a relic for you," he whispered.

"A relic?"

"Sshh," said Paul. "They didn't know its value," he said. "But our agent did."

Kline caught a brief movement out of the corner of his eye. He turned to the doorway to see another man standing there, one hand missing, hair blond. He was frowning.

"Ah," said Kline. "You must be Paul."

The Paul beside him stiffened. He lifted the breakfast tray and hurried out. The Paul in the doorway moved to let him past, then followed him out, pushing the door shut behind him.

Another Paul came in a few hours later to bring him lunch, then another Paul not long afterward who changed his dressings and massaged his legs and helped him up to the bathroom. Neither were talkative, both answering his questions simply and noncommittally. Yes, they were each called Paul. Yes, they both had had other names, dead names, but both were firm in their refusal to divulge them. No, he was not a prisoner, they claimed, but they both encouraged him so strongly to remain in bed that he felt as if he were a prisoner. To the question "What am I doing here?" and the question "What do you want from me?"—each posed to a different Paul—they just smiled. All, they assured him, would be explained in time. "By whom?" he asked, and was not surprised when they answered, "By Paul."

After the last Paul was gone, he tried to think. Could he make his way out without them stopping him? His shoulder still throbbed when he moved that side of his body. His head hurt too, but the knife was mostly gone from his eye, and when it came was not nearly as severe, as if it were stabbing into a wound whose edges had already been cauterized, was just slightly tearing the fleshy edge of his brain. He was hardly at his best, but he was far from his worst. Was he in good enough shape to leave?

Over the course of the day, the paintings started to feel familiar, no longer so strange. True, they were grotesque, but it became harder and harder to keep that in mind. The screaming or singing man started to seem more and more incidental to the composition of the picture as a whole, and he found himself thinking about the pattern of ochres and blacks and clammy whites, about the cast of light and shadow, in a way he almost found soothing.

A Paul came in, a new one or a repeater, he wasn't sure. They had all started to look alike to him. The Paul held a dinner tray. Kline ate slowly. He was, he told himself, feeling much better.

"Paul," he said.

"Yes?" said Paul.

"I don't suppose you'd care to tell me what's going on here?"

"That is not for me to say," said Paul.

"I suppose not," said Kline. "I should wait for Paul then, should I?"

Paul beamed, nodded. "Soon," he said. "No need to worry."

After Paul was gone, Kline lay thinking. He could get out of bed and when one of the Pauls came, as long as he was not a large Paul, he could probably feign weakness and then, while the Paul was unsuspecting, overpower him. He would hit him in the throat as hard as he could, or almost: not hard enough to kill him. Would it be hard enough? Would it be too hard? He kept thinking about it, imagining his hand flashing out, how the Paul's throat would feel to the blade of it, of the hand.

But no, he realized, he was now too curious to leave before finding out more about what was going on.

◆ ◆ ◆

That night he had dreams of conflagration, scattered bits and fragments of burnings that seemed, he reflected later, to be assembled from many moments of smoke or fire, benign or otherwise, that he had experienced in his life. Yet in the midst of the fragments was a single roaring kernel: he saw himself, arm missing to the elbow, stumble out of a doorway and shoot a gun-handed guard through the head. *This is a dream*, he told himself, and was pleased that he could recognize this, though later there came gradually a nagging suspicion that it was not *just* a dream, had not always been a dream.

He shot the guard through the head and the man fell back gasping, hissing blood through his lips in a fine mist that slowly shadowed the floor beside his face. After a little while, the fellow seemed dead. Kline searched his pockets, found cigarettes, a book of matches. He used the matches to light the dead man's clothing on fire, then stood watching, making sure the flames started feeding up the wall.

Doors near him started to open and then quickly closed again. People were shouting. He stumbled his way down the stairs and shot a guard coming up, a lucky shot this time. A few seconds later he tripped over the man's body and fell the rest of the way down.

When he awoke it was to a man playing the piano, a careful, melancholy piece. He could only see the man from the back but could still tell he was blond and missing a hand. A Paul, certainly. He was playing one-handed but the piece didn't seem to be suffering as a result.

The piece slowed further, wound around itself, slowly died. The man stayed at the instrument, pedal down, letting the last notes resonate. One hand and half his body was hunched over the keyboard. The other arm, the stump, hung loosely at his side, as if each half of his body was controlled by a different brain. It was a curious and startling effect.

Eventually the notes faded utterly and both halves of the man's back finally relaxed to become a single back again. He swiveled around to regard Kline.

"Hindemith," he said. "Wittgenstein commissioned it—not the philosopher but his musical brother, Paul, who'd lost his arm in the war. He commissioned more than half a hundred one-handed piano pieces. He was a visionary."

Not knowing what else to say, Kline said: "Paul, I presume."

"Indeed," said the man, smiling slightly. Standing, he came to Kline's bedside.

"But you haven't always been called Paul, have you," said Kline.

"Perhaps the most successful of the pieces Paul Wittgenstein commissioned, philosophically speaking, is another one by Hindemith, which is a struggle even for a two-handed man to play well. And yet there is something about the stress it places on the fingers of the one-handed man that gives it a poignancy that a more relaxed, more confident two-handed approach is virtually unable to bring about. Hindemith had two hands, but when he wrote that piece it was as if he had only one. Do you play, friend Kline?"

"Play what?"

"The piano, of course," said the Paul.

"No," said Kline.

"Never learned?" said the Paul. "Took childhood lessons but never followed through?"

"Something like that," said Kline.

The Paul went back to the piano and struck a chord, let it resonate, then struck its tonic inverse.

"I of course have the advantage on you," said the Paul. "I've had my eyes on you for quite some time. You, on the other hand, have little if any idea who I am."

"You're Paul," said Kline.

"Who isn't?" asked the Paul. "Even you might well be Paul, were there not another role prepared for you."

"Who says I want to accept it?" said Kline.

"Surely you don't believe, friend Kline, that we have any choice in the paths our lives take? God is the only one who controls our fate. We are predestined from the beginning. You believe in God, don't you?"

Kline didn't answer.

"No matter," said the Paul. "It makes no difference whether you believe in God, since God, so I have been led to understand, believes in you. And we believe in you as well, friend Kline. At first we weren't sure you were the one, so we watched. But now we're sure. From the moment you chose to go with their messengers to the compound, your fate has ground itself inexorably forward."

"Who's we?"

"We," said the Paul, and spread his arms wide. "Paul."

"I'm not the one, Paul," said Kline. "Whatever it is, I'm not it."

"But you are," said the Paul.

Kline shook his head.

"You made us certain when, instead of being killed by them, you extricated yourself wielding a sword of destruction. Metaphorically, I mean. By a sword I mean a gun."

"Like hell," said Kline.

"Yes," said Paul. "Exactly like hell. You harrowed them."

"I want to leave now," said Kline. He tried to look away, but didn't know where else to look.

Paul frowned. "You can go," he said. "You always could. We're not like them. Nobody is stopping you from going. But they'll be looking for you. Borchert's men."

"That so?" said Kline.

"They'll never stop looking," said Paul. "It's either you or them. An eye for an eye, friend Kline. If you leave, you'll have to kill them all."

They left him alone in the room for the rest of the day, though he had the feeling that if he were to get out of bed and go toward the door a Paul would suddenly be there, attentive, perhaps more than one. He could, he thought, leave if he needed to. He felt all right, considering, would be all right if leaving was all it was. But despite their assurances that he was free to go, he couldn't believe they wouldn't try to stop him. And once he was out, if Borchert's men came after him, what then? Better to stay and recover as best he could, choose the right moment to leave.

The trick, he told himself, was to avoid letting his curiosity get the better of his judgment, to know when, still suffering or no, to leave. He looked again at the painting of the one-legged screamer and now it seemed to him that the man wanted to leave the scene but couldn't, couldn't bring himself to limp out on the bleeding woman bundled up beside him, perhaps dead. Perhaps that was why he was screaming.

But I'm not like him, Kline told himself. *If I have to leave something behind, I do. Even when it's part of me.*

His dinner was brought to him by the piano-playing Paul, the Paul that seemed to be in charge. It consisted of a scoop of mashed potatoes, skins worked in, and a chicken leg.

"You're still here," the Paul said.

Kline nodded.

"I'm glad you decided to stay," said the Paul. "Things have gone so nicely to this point that I'd hate for them to take an unfortunate turn now."

"I'm not the one," said Kline. "Whatever it is you think I am, I'm not it."

"How can you say so if you don't even know what it is, friend Kline? You have to give yourself a chance."

Kline just shook his head.

"There's something I want to show you," said the Paul.

He turned slightly toward the open doorway and in came another Paul, carrying before him a lacquered casket, about a foot and a half long, fairly narrow. He carried it carefully forward and presented it to the first Paul, who took it and then carefully placed it on the bed, balancing it in Kline's lap.

"Go ahead," he said to Kline, "open it."

"What's in it?" asked Kline.

"Open it," he said again.

The casket had a gilt hasp, firmly shut but not locked. He ran his hand over the lacquered wood; it was smooth, felt exactly as it looked.

Undoing the hasp with the edge of his thumb, he opened the lid. The casket was lined with red velvet, the angle of the light lending it an odd sheen. The only thing in the box was a bone. Or rather two bones, from a forearm or foreleg, held together by a strand of wire at each end. He reached in and touched them, then glanced over at Paul.

"Go ahead," Paul said. "Pick it up if you want."

"What is it?" asked Kline.

"A relic," said Paul.

When he lifted the bones out, they clicked against one another. They were, he was suddenly certain, human. Both had been sheared off, leaving the ends open and porous and, he saw, strangely dark. He leaned the bones against the box and prodded the end of one; the marrow gave slightly, was oddly spongy.

"These are recent," said Kline, slightly surprised.

"Of course they are," said Paul. "They belonged to you."

Kline pulled back his hand, as if stung.

"We have one of our best Pauls seeing what he can do about acquiring your toes. We'd like your hand as well, but we've been looking for that for much longer and inquiries seem to have led nowhere. You wouldn't happen to know where it went, would you? Kept in evidence, perhaps?"

"Please," said Kline, "please, take it away."

The Paul stopped and looked at him closely. "There's nothing to worry about, friend Kline," he said. "Every bone has to come from somewhere. This one just happens to have come from you." He reached out and carefully lifted the bones, settled them into the casket, closed the lid. "It has a life of its own now, friend Kline."

"Thank God," said Kline.

The Paul stooped and awkwardly gathered the casket up, settling it on his forearms and carrying it out before him.

"Besides," he said. "It's not just you. We all have relics. I could show you my own if you'd like."

"Somehow that doesn't reassure me," said Kline.

"Would you like to see it?" asked the Paul.

"Absolutely not," said Kline.

"Don't worry," said the Paul. "You'll get used to it. You'll even start to understand it. You won't be able to help yourself." He started toward the door. "Some other time, then," he said, and went out.

Kline closed his eyes but against his eyelids still saw the bone, its spongy end. He opened them again, stared at the piano, the lacquered sheen of it.

The trick, he told himself, *is knowing when to leave, and then leaving.* And then he thought, *I have to leave now.*

II.

He lay in bed pretending to be asleep, waiting. Every so often he heard a shuffling and one of the Pauls came to the door, peered in, eyes blurry, then shuffled away. He let that happen six times and then the seventh time got up just after the Paul had left and began to search the room.

The top drawer of a mahogany tallboy contained a neat stack of undershirts and an even neater stack of boxers and a robe. He awkwardly struggled out of his gown, stump throbbing, and into an undershirt. The boxers he spread out on the floor and then stepped into the leg-holes, pulling them up around his hips with his single hand. They were a little big but would do. He slipped the robe on.

He tried the other drawers of the tallboy, found them all empty. He searched around the room for a pair of pants, finding nothing of note except, beneath the bathroom sink, a barrage of cleaning supplies and, wrapped in an old towel, a bedpan. This latter he took out and hefted. It was a little awkward but then he realized he could slip his hand into it and make a fist and it would stay in place when he swung it back and forth.

When a Paul came to the door for the eighth time and saw the bed empty, he took a step forward and was struck in the face by a bedpan. It hurt Kline's hand quite a bit, but seemed to hurt the Paul a great deal more. The Paul stumbled and started to go down and then began to catch himself, groping at one of his pockets with his stump. Kline hit him again, on the side of the head this time, and he went down for good.

Kline worked his hand out of the bedpan and let it drop and then started to slip the Paul's pants off. There was blood coming out of the Paul's mouth, he realized, and he opened his mouth to see the Paul had bitten through his tongue. He turned the head a little so as to keep him from choking to death on his own blood, then fished the severed tip out of the mouth and laid it on the carpet beside his head.

Like a slug, he thought, working the Paul's pants the rest of the way off. There was nothing in the pants pockets. He took off his robe and tried the pants on and they didn't fit, they were too tight, so he stepped out of them and put the robe back on.

He imagined the other Pauls coming in to find this Paul unconscious, his severed tongue arranged neatly beside him. And then he realized, his body instantly feeling heavier, they would see the tongue and then do one of two things. Either they would all cut off their own tongues, making all the Pauls identical again, or they would make a holy relic of this tongue.

He picked the tongue up, carried it into the bathroom, and flushed it down the toilet.

He moved down a dim hall, past first one open doorway and then a second, each opening onto rooms that, as far as he could tell in the dim light, were like his own. The hall turned abruptly to the right and then terminated in a T-intersection. He turned right, went past another doorway and into growing darkness. When it became too difficult to see, he stopped and traced his steps back, taking the left fork.

He followed this down to another T-intersection, then followed the right branch, where there seemed to be more light, and came to a heavy banister and a spiral staircase. The light was coming from below. He leaned over the banister and saw, standing perhaps fifteen feet below, a Paul.

He started down the stairs, moving slowly, watching the Paul. The man just stood there, wearing a light jacket, arms crossed, facing a large door. Kline went silently around another turn of the stairs and then leaned far over the banister and struck the Paul hard over the head with the bedpan.

The Paul took a step and then sat down, the back of his head slowly darkening with blood. Then he slumped over bonelessly.

Kline came down the rest of the way and searched the Paul's pockets. The pocket of his jacket had a gun in it and a ten-dollar bill and a car key on a rubber band.

Kline took everything, then started for the door. It was locked.

He looked at the key again, even tried it but, no, he knew it was a car key not a door key: it didn't fit. When he turned around to try to figure out what to do next, there was the chief Paul sitting on the bottom step of the stairs, watching him.

"Anything the matter?" the Paul asked.

Kline lifted the pistol, pointed it at him.

"Friend Kline," the Paul said. "You sadden me."

"Where's the key to the door?" demanded Kline.

"Nobody here has the key, friend Kline," said the Paul. He spread his arms, displayed his stump and an open palm. "There's no need for any of this."

"How do you get out if there's no key?"

"I don't want to get out," said the Paul. "Paul is perfectly happy where he is." He pointed at the gun with his stump. "No need for that," he said. "Please, put it away."

Kline looked at the gun, then shrugged, let it slowly fall to his side. "All right," he said.

"There," said the Paul. "Don't you feel much better now that we can talk this over like civilized adults?"

"I want to leave," said Kline.

"If you really wanted to leave, all you had to do was ask," said the Paul. He stood and came slowly toward Kline, then moved past him and to the door. "Ask and ye shall receive," he said, "knock and it shall be opened unto you." He knocked twice, waited, then knocked a third time.

"What is wanted?" asked a muffled voice from the other side.

"Kline, having been true and faithful in all things, desires to turn his face away from the Lord by entering the lone and dreary world."

"Present him at the door and his request shall be granted," said the voice.

The Paul motioned him forward, positioned him in front of the door. He knocked once, then waited, then knocked twice more.

There was a rustling on the other side and the lock clicked. The door opened and Kline found himself looking into what appeared to be an empty building lobby, brightly lit. A revolving door on the far side opened onto a dark street. Beside it stood a Paul wearing a doorman's uniform.

"You see, friend Kline? We're men of our word. You're free to go."

Kline nodded, stepped forward and past the doorman.

"You took Paul's key, friend Kline, and his gun," said the chief Paul from behind. "There was no need to knock him out."

"I'm sorry," said Kline warily, holding out the key.

"No, no," said the chief Paul, waving his stump. "You might as well keep it. Paul's car is parked just outside, isn't it Paul?" he said, looking at the doorman. The doorman nodded. "It's a mistake to leave," said the chief Paul. "They'll kill you," he said. "But we all of us have to make our own mistakes. We all of us have free agency, friend Kline. But far be it from me to force a man to go on foot to his own death. By all means, take the car."

"Thank you," said Kline.

"You sure you won't reconsider?" asked the Paul.

Kline shook his head and moved through the door.

"A pity, friend Kline," he heard from behind him. "I was certain you were the one."

He tried the key in three car doors before it opened the door of a rusted, lime-green Ford Pinto. He climbed in, only now starting to feel how exhausted he was.

He cursed when he realized the car was a standard. He started it in neutral and then shifted it into first, slowly working the steering wheel around with his solitary hand until the wheels jacked sharply out. He could feel pressure in his clutch foot, the toes reminding him of their absence. Not pain exactly, though there was pain too, in his armless shoulder as he moved his other arm. He let out the clutch and the car lurched out, just nicking the bumper of the car ahead of him but scraping past. And then he had his hands, or rather his hand, full trying to correct before plowing into the cars on the other side of the street.

He drove slowly, releasing the steering wheel to shift up or down. After a few minutes, he managed to scoot forward so as to hold the wheel steady with his knee when shifting, and then it was a little easier.

It wasn't a town he knew. He drove around until he came to the marker for a state road, took it. He followed the state road to another state road and then followed that to the interstate, took that south toward home.

It had just started to get light when he realized he was almost out of gas. He took the next exit, went to a Conoco just off the freeway. It was closed. He went to the next exit, found an all-night truck stop, pulled the car in. He pumped in ten dollars of gas, then went inside to pay.

The attendant, old and grizzled, looked oddly at his dressing gown and his missing arm. Kline held out his ten dollars.

"Couldn't sleep?" said the attendant, gesturing at the gown.

"Something like that," said Kline.

"Cops were looking for someone a few days back," the attendant said. "Description matched you, more or less. Don't suppose it lines up with all that many folks."

A trucker in the candy aisle had started staring at them. Kline began to feel very tired.

"Can't be too easy to drive like that," the attendant said.

Kline shrugged.

"Say the man's a killer," said the attendant.

"Just a misunderstanding," said Kline.

"None of my business," said the attendant, "but seems to me a man who's a killer wouldn't bother to pay for his gas." He reached out and took the ten from Kline's hand and Kline saw he was missing a thumb. "Besides, they aren't even offering no reward. Good luck to you," the attendant said, and Kline made for the door.

He drove for a while on back roads, just in case, but after a half hour or so he realized that if he kept it up he wouldn't make it on the gas he had. The sun rose hot and dry and began to burn through the car. He rolled down the window but became worried that the drag would take up too much gas, so he rolled it back up, turned on the vent, slowly started to sweat.

He made it to the exit to his city and then to the city limits, the car lurching up the last few hills but kicking in again on the way down. Almost a half-mile from his apartment it died for good. He left it there half-blocking the street and set out on foot. The sidewalks had a modest scattering of people on them, late risers or people late for work or people out for other reasons. He tried not to look at them as he limped past in his bathrobe, though many stopped to look at him. He kept going, stopping once in a doorway to catch his breath.

It wasn't until he was at the building door, barely able to stand, that he realized he didn't have his key. He pushed the buzzer for the super's apartment, then sat down on the steps to wait. When there was no answer, he depressed the buzzer again, holding it down until the door buzzed and he finally could push his way in.

The super was waiting just inside the second door, hands on his hips, mustache bristling, eyes bleary, lips pursed. When he saw Kline his anger fled, was replaced by something uneasy, much less sure of itself.

"It's you," he said. "You came back."

"I don't have my key," said Kline. He was so exhausted, he was having difficulty standing.

"What happened?" asked the super.

"Two men kidnapped me," said Kline. "After that, things started getting weird. I meant to come back sooner. Is it the rent you're worried about?"

But the super had his forearms up, as if defending himself from blows. "No," he was saying, "I meant your arm."

"Oh," said Kline. "I lost it."

The super opened his mouth and closed it again. He went back into his apartment and got the master key, then helped Kline up the stairs and to his door, opening it for him.

"I'll have a new key made for you," said the super, "next day or so. Until then, you'll have to talk to me to get in."

Kline nodded and stumbled his way in. Everything, he noticed dimly, was covered in a layer of fine dust. And then he was on the bed, and already, despite the sudden pain in his shoulder, in his eye, mostly asleep.

III.

When he awoke, the room was dark. Confused, he looked first for the hospital curtain and then for the two grotesque paintings, but found nothing. There was only a blank white wall, a man's shadow cast upon it. The shadow moved and he turned his head to find himself suddenly looking at Frank, two uniformed cops standing just behind him.

"Seems like I'm always waiting for you to wake up," said Frank.

Kline just blinked.

"If I had a cigarette, this would be the moment I lit it and smoked it while waiting for you to say something," said Frank. "Only I don't smoke."

"No?" said Kline.

"No," said Frank. "And besides, I want things to go quicker this time around."

"Why didn't you wake me?"

"We tried," said Frank. "I shook you and shouted and slapped you around a little, but it didn't help. I tried to convince these boys in blue behind me to see if their kisses would awaken you. But no matter how impatient we were, we just had to wait."

"How'd you find me?"

"If you thought about it even for a moment you wouldn't have to ask," said Frank. "One word. Super."

Kline nodded.

"Enough fun and games," said Frank, and Kline watched his expression shift just slightly, face growing hard, pupils shrinking to dots, gaze steadying. "Let's hear about it."

"Hear about what?"

His eyes grew harder. He took an unsharpened pencil from his pocket and turned it absently between his fingers. He stood and leaned in over the bed, resting a heavy hand on Kline's shoulder. The other hand brought the pencil up near Kline's eye, then moved it toward his temple. Then he moved it down and pressed its end against the dressings over the bullet wound.

At first it was just a gentle pressure, an odd and nervous reminder of its own presence, but then Frank pushed harder, and the vision in one of Kline's eyes began to fold in on itself and go out. He felt the knife dart back again, deep again in his eye, the pain starting to build. He closed his eyes and waited to pass out.

As suddenly as it had started the pressure vanished. When he opened his eyes again, Frank was back in his chair, twirling the pencil between his fingers, watching him.

"Let's hear about it," said Frank.

"Hear about what?" Kline asked.

Then Frank was standing again, his hand against Kline's shoulder and pressing him down into the bed. He was holding the pencil between his teeth and had a pocketknife in one hand and had begun to cut through the dressings over Kline's shoulder. Once he was through, he carefully folded the knife and put it back into his pocket, then took the pencil and pressed its end against Kline's stump.

It made Kline's eye hurt first and then it hurt inside his shoulder too and somehow in his throat so that he wanted to cough. And then Frank pushed very hard and the shoulder seared with pain and God's knife flashed all the way through his skull and out the hole in the back and he stopped being able to think and blacked out.

When he opened his eyes again, Frank was back in his chair, calm, twirling the pencil around between his fingers. Behind him, the two cops looked worried. The end of the pencil was now slick with blood. His shoulder throbbed.

"Let's hear about it," said Frank.

"This could go on all day," said Kline.

"It doesn't have to," said Frank. "It all depends on you."

They stared at each other.

"All right," said Kline finally. "What do you want to know?"

They started with Davis, his murder, Kline telling the truth and then Frank prodding one wound or the other until he was convinced it was actually the truth and there was no more to tell. At the beginning Kline kept thinking he could lie if he wanted to, but as blood began to drip off the pencil he realized that no, probably he couldn't, not now, not convincingly.

"That hurt me worse than it hurt you," said Frank, and smiled. Kline watched the two uniformed officers behind him exchange glances. "I'm a peace-loving man. I tried to do this the easy way, but you weren't interested."

"I'm starting to get interested," said Kline, eyes following the pencil.

"That was then," said Frank. "We're past that now. You know what the difference is? Davis being dead, for one. Not that he was much of a cop, but he didn't deserve to die."

"I didn't kill him," said Kline.

"No," said Frank. "We'd basically determined that. Technically speaking, you didn't kill him. But what I want to know is why the man who was missing an arm and could hardly move, let alone walk, is alive while the police officer with all his limbs is dead?"

"I don't know," said Kline.

"You don't know," said Frank, and leaned forward.

"No," said Kline quickly. "I do know. He fell asleep."

"He fell asleep?"

"I didn't sleep."

"Does that seem fair to you, Mr. Kline?"

"I don't even know what fair means," said Kline. "Why aren't we having this conversation at the station?"

"I have a reputation to maintain," said Frank. One of the officers behind him looked even more nervous. "I don't want people getting the wrong idea."

He reached out and pushed the pencil's end against Kline's stump, twisting it slightly.

Kline winced. "What do you want to know now?" he asked.

Frank looked up, smiled. "Who says I want to know anything?" he asked, and pushed harder.

And then, just as the knife was pushing its way into his eye again, the world burst apart. The door burst open and a man with a gun in place of a hand stood there and there was a rattling and one policeman's head came quickly open to reveal what was inside. The other policeman had his gun partway out and was half-crouched and turning, and then the rattling came again and he jerked about and his side split open and he shot twice into the floor, spun about, and fell.

Frank had dived out the closed window and now flailed about on the fire escape, face and hands cut up by the glass, trying to free his gun from its holster. The mutilate took a few steps toward him and raised his gun prosthesis again and a look of amazement crossed Frank's face. He threw himself sideways, the bullets thudding into the window casement and sparking off the railing of the fire escape. Kline heard him falling or stumbling down the stairs, away.

The guard looked at Kline, who hadn't moved, and smiled.

"We've found you, Mr. Kline," he said. He pointed his gun prosthesis at Kline, gestured. "Up," he said. "Time to go."

Kline stood, raised his hands. The guard kept his distance, always training the gun on him, following him from behind and to the side, always there in the corner of Kline's vision.

"Open the door and take two steps into the hall," the guard said. "Slowly."

He did as he was told, the guard just behind him. The hall was empty except for people standing near their doors, watching his door.

"What do you see?" the guard asked, closer behind him now.

"What's going on?" asked a man three doors down.

"My neighbors," said Kline.

"No police?" he said.

"No," said Kline.

"Tell them to go back inside," said the guard.

"Go back inside," said Kline.

"What's going on?" the man said again.

"Nothing's going on," said Kline.

"I thought I heard shots," the man said.

The guard pushed Kline forward, almost making him stumble down. "Go back inside," he heard the guard say, and half-turned to see the guard pointing his gun-arm at the neighbor. *This is the moment,* Kline fleetingly thought, *if this were a film I'd knock the guard's arm upward and overpower him.* But Kline was twisted the wrong way around; the gun was on the same side as his missing arm.

He heard a door close, saw that the neighbor had disappeared.

"All right," said the guard. "Down the stairs."

He started for the door to the back stairs but the guard gestured him away, pointed toward the front.

"This way, Mr. Kline," he said. "We don't have anything to be ashamed of. We're going out the front door."

He went slowly, wondering with each step if another chance would come. He listened to the guard behind. The man's steps were careful and regular, no hesitation to them.

The gun jabbed into his back. "Hurry up," the guard said. "Make it quick."

He sped up a little, stumbled again, caught himself, then continued down the stairs. In the lobby was another mutilate, a man missing both ears, several fingers, most of his palm. He was pacing back and forth nervously. He had a gun but held it awkwardly—as if he'd never seen a gun before, let alone used one.

"Hurry it up!" he shouted when he saw them. "Hurry it up!"

"Where's the cop, John?" asked the guard, looking through the glass doors onto the street.

"What cop?" asked John, gaze darting nervously about.

"Never mind," said the guard. "Out the front door, John," he said. "After you, Mr. Kline."

Kline pushed the door open then lifted his hand back up above his head and went out. The light outside was brighter than he'd imagined. It confused him for a moment.

"Straight ahead," hissed the guard. "Black car. Back door. Run."

He saw the black car, double-parked just across the street, and made for it, John moaning with fear beside him. He reached the car and pulled the door open and threw himself in, John right after him and nearly on top of him, the guard right after that. "Go, go!" John was yelling to the driver, but the driver didn't move and when the guard prodded him the man's head fell to one side and a red gash gaped at his throat. John started to scream, a high-pitched sound, and then the window beside Kline cracked and went opaque and John was dead, the front of his face gone. The guard tried to get his gun-arm around, knocking it against the seat in front of him, and then the rear window cracked and went opaque and his head burst brightly over the headrest in front of him. The gun rattled briefly, slugs thumping through the ceiling, and then stopped.

The door opened and there was Frank, eyes still hard, looking unblinkingly at him, gashed and bloody, breathing heavily.

"I should kill you now," he said. "Save us all a lot of trouble."

"I wish you wouldn't," said Kline.

"Come on," said Frank wearily. "Get out."

Kline slowly climbed over the dead guard, trying not to touch him. He was still managing it when he heard a shot and Frank gave a little cry. Kline slid the rest of the way out and crouched, shielding himself behind the car door. Frank was there too, on one knee, one arm hanging limply as if it were no longer alive. The other arm was trying to aim the gun, failing. He tried to stand but seemed to be having trouble.

Another shot rang out and Frank was knocked down. Kline stayed crouched, wondering if he should try to run or if he should crawl back into the car. In the distance, faintly, sirens. He got his legs under him and got ready to run but instead just stayed there, waiting. *What's wrong with me?* he wondered. Frank lay on the sidewalk, coughing blood, still alive.

He would run across the street, he told himself, back toward the building. Or rather he would start running, he corrected himself, and then be shot dead.

He got ready to go, tensed himself, but couldn't bring himself to run. Instead he slowly stood and stepped out from behind the car door. He stopped long enough to tilt Frank's head slightly, to keep him from choking to death on his own blood, and then straightened himself and stood, waiting for them to kill him.

Only they didn't kill him. Instead, they came out from behind a car. There were two of them, and they were both smiling even though the one with the gun kept it trained on him. Kline knew them both: Gous and Ramse.

"We've come full circle, Mr. Kline," said Ramse, moving toward him.

"Seems fitting, no?" said Gous.

"We knew the place," said Ramse, "having gotten you the first time. So, we were the logical choice."

"So, back in favor," said Gous.

They got close enough for Ramse to prod Frank with his boot.

"Poor bastard," said Gous.

"He deserved it," said Ramse.

"He was just doing his job," said Gous. "His only mistake was not realizing there was a second car. There's always a second car. Except when there's not." He gestured with his gun at Kline. "By all rights this should be our friend Kline."

Ramse shrugged. "That's Kline," he said. "We know and love him. He's like a person to us."

"More or less," said Gous.

"Yes," said Ramse. "More or less." He prodded Frank again with his foot. "What do you think, Gous? Shall we kill him?"

"No point overdoing it," said Gous.

"No," said Ramse. "I suppose not. Besides, we should be going."

"We should indeed," said Gous. The sirens, Kline suddenly realized, sounded quite near. "Into the car, Mr. Kline," he said, gesturing behind him with his gun. "Time to go."

He sat in the front seat. Ramse drove by placing his stump in the cup attached to the steering wheel, while Gous in the backseat trained the gun at Kline's back or his head, sometimes one, sometimes the other.

They passed a police car, siren flailing, going the other way. Ramse didn't even give it a glance, didn't seem at all nervous.

"Back to the compound?" asked Kline.

"Back to the compound," said Ramse, and smiled.

They drove through the suburbs, signs of habitation slowly giving way to dry, withered trees.

"They're planning to kill me?" asked Kline.

"Yes," said Ramse. "We."

"What?" asked Kline.

"We're planning to kill you," said Ramse. "Slowly and painfully. We're part of them."

"It's semantic," said Gous. "There's no point correcting him."

"We know him, Gous," said Ramse, watching his friend in the rearview mirror. "He's shifty. He's trying to draw a line between us and the others."

"So?" said Gous.

"So, we have to watch ourselves," said Ramse. "We have to be on guard."

"I don't think it's that big of a deal," said Gous. "We're smarter than that."

They kept arguing back and forth about it, and then Ramse shouted, and then finally, both furious, they refused to speak to one another. The sun slipped down in the sky and disappeared, the car and the landscape it traveled through cast now in an orange light, as if everything were slightly underexposed. When the light was completely gone, Ramse asked him to reach across him and turn on the headlights. He thought fleetingly about jerking the steering wheel and trying to crash the car, but before he'd even started to reach he felt the snout of Gous' pistol push into the nape of his neck. "Careful now," Gous said.

He reached slowly across and pushed in the light button and fell back again. Gous' pistol wavered for a moment beside his ear, then darted away. They kept driving.

"I'm sorry," said Gous to Ramse. "I didn't mean to say anything to hurt you."

"I'm the one that's sorry," said Ramse. "There's no reason to fight."

Kline rolled his eyes. They kept driving. Kline felt like he should recognize the road, but, in the dark, didn't. "Why do they want us to bring him back?" said Gous. "They're just going to kill him. Why don't we just kill him ourselves?"

"They're not just going to kill him," said Ramse. "They're planning to crucify him." He leaned over to Kline. "Sorry," he said, "but you might as well know."

"It's all right," said Kline.

"If it was our choice," said Gous, "it might turn out differently."

"But it's not our choice," said Ramse.

"I understand," said Kline.

"Very kind of you," said Gous. "You always were considerate."

"Don't overdo it, Gous," said Ramse.

"Sorry," said Gous.

"It's the thought that counts," Kline offered.

"I hope so," said Ramse, "because there's nothing beyond that."

"No?" asked Kline.

"No," said Ramse.

"Ah well," said Kline. "I had a good run."

But he wasn't thinking that. What he was thinking was, *When do I try to crash the car?*

The city had faded entirely behind him, miles back. The road was dark and deserted. *When?* he wondered. *When?* But every time he felt almost ready, he felt the presence of Gous' pistol just behind his ear.

"What are you?" Ramse asked after a few dozen miles. "A four still?"

Kline thought it over. "Yes," he said.

"But it's the whole arm," said Ramse. "Shouldn't it count for more? See what I'm saying? Shouldn't an arm count more than a hand?"

"I don't know," said Kline.

"Sure," said Ramse. "And shouldn't a hand count more than a few fingers?"

"Ramse," said Gous. "You know that's not how it's done."

"I'm not challenging the doctrine," said Ramse. "I'm still faithful. I'm just asking."

They drove for a time in silence. After a while, almost without knowing it, Kline dropped off, jerking awake some time later when they turned down a dirt road.

"Almost there," said Ramse when he realized that Kline was awake again.

They went down the dirt road, the car jouncing with each dip and bump.

"It's nothing personal," said Ramse. "Gous and I both like you."

"Yes," said Gous. "We do."

"But we have our orders," said Ramse.

Gous didn't say anything.

Kline said, "I'd prefer not to die."

"No," said Ramse, distracted. "But we all die when it's our time."

Gous was still there, still always alert. *I'm running out of time*, Kline thought. He would have to reach over, pistol or no, and pull the steering wheel sharply, try to jam his foot onto the accelerator as well. How much time was there?

"Almost there," said Ramse. "Mr. Kline," he said, "I have nothing but regrets."

"Then let me go," said Kline.

"Ah," said Ramse. "If only we could. But alas we cannot."

"Speak for yourself, Ramse," said Gous.

"Excuse me?" said Ramse. His eyes flicked up to the rearview mirror, then his face went slack. "You wouldn't," he said.

Kline half-turned to see the gun pointed no longer at himself, but at Ramse.

"I wouldn't like to," said Gous. "Pull over."

Ramse took his foot off the accelerator an instant, then put it back again. "What's this all about, Gous?" he asked.

Gous rapped him sharply on the shoulder with the butt of his gun. "Pull over, Ramse," he said. This time Ramse complied, letting the car grind slowly to a stop and then, on Gous' command, handing over the keys.

"I can't say I'm not hurt, Gous," said Ramse. "After all we've been to each other."

"It hurts me more than it hurts you, Ramse," said Gous. "Now suppose we all get out," he said. "I'll go first, then Mr. Kline, then finally you, dear Ramse."

The car swayed slightly as Gous made his way out, leaving the door open. "Now you, Kline," he said, and Kline opened his door and climbed out as well. "In front of the car," said Gous. "In the lights. Put your hand on the hood and wait."

Kline nodded and did as he was told, looking in at Ramse who was pale and silent, lips tight. The hood was warm under his palm.

"Now you, Ramse," said Gous. "Right beside friend Kline."

"You're planning to kill me?" said Ramse.

"Why would I want to kill you?" asked Gous. "I have no desire to kill you. But yes, if you don't get out now, I'll have to kill you."

"You'll kill me anyway," said Ramse.

Gous sighed. "Ramse, don't you know me better than that?"

"Apparently I don't know you at all."

Gous gestured impatiently with the gun. "Ramse," he said, "please."

Ramse sighed and clambered out.

"Turn around and raise your stumps," Gous said, and when Ramse did so he stepped quickly forward and struck him in the head with the butt-end of the pistol.

Ramse crumpled quickly. Gous prodded him with his foot, then came back to the car.

"You'll have to drive," said Gous. "Get in."

Kline did, and Gous clambered in beside him, looking suddenly worn and tired.

"Think you can manage?" he asked.

"I can manage," said Kline.

He reached across and turned the key, then awkwardly levered the car into drive, started slowly forward.

"Try not to hit Ramse," said Gous.

"All right," said Kline, and turned the wheel a little more sharply.

Gous pointed and Kline spun the car awkwardly around, almost driving it into the ditch. He got it straightened out, let himself go faster.

They drove in silence for the better part of an hour, Kline letting his gaze flit occasionally over to Gous, who hardly moved.

"What's this all about, Gous?" Kline finally asked.

"Please," said Gous. "Call me Paul."

IV.

How much weirder, thought Kline, *is it possible for my life to get?* And then he pushed the thought down and tried to ignore it, afraid of what the answer might be.

They stopped for gas and Kline thought briefly about making a break for it, but Gous stayed right beside him, gun hidden in the pocket of his jacket, as he pumped the gas and then took the money Gous gave him inside to pay. He was still in his robe, but it was dirtier now, and bloodstained. The attendant looked them over carefully as he took the money. He couldn't stop himself, before they were even completely out the door, from reaching for the telephone.

"Ah hell," said Gous, rolling his eyes and turning around long enough to shoot him.

"You'd think he'd have at least some discretion," said Gous on the way back out. "You'd think he'd at least wait until we'd gotten in the car."

"Did you kill him?" asked Kline.

"Probably," said Gous.

"What if he was only calling his girlfriend?" asked Kline as they climbed in and started to drive.

Gous gave him a disgusted look. "Why would you say that to me? Are you trying to make me feel bad?"

"I'm sorry," said Kline, surprised.

"What's done is done," said Gous.

"What exactly is it that's being done, Gous?" asked Kline.

"Paul," said Gous, absently. "Call me Paul."

◆ ◆ ◆

They drove for some time in silence.

"How'd you become involved with the Pauls?" asked Kline finally.

"The usual way," said Gous.

Kline said nothing.

"I was a one," Gous said. "I'd cut off the proper hand, joined the brotherhood. Then I was approached. What Paul had to say seemed to me correct. It struck a chord."

"But you're no longer a one," said Kline.

"No," said Gous. "They needed someone on the inside. After a while it became clear I'd have to have additional amputations or else become suspect." He turned toward Kline. "I'm still a Paul," he said. "Only more so."

Gous had him pull off the freeway and into a small town, kept giving him instructions on where to turn.

"Of course I've rendered them a few invaluable services," said Gous. "It doesn't take a genius to see that."

Kline didn't say anything, just kept driving. After a while things looked vaguely familiar. Soon after, Gous had him pull to a stop beneath a streetlamp and they got out, walking half a block to the lobby of the Pauls' compound. The doorman raised his missing hand in greeting.

"Well met, Paul," said Gous.

"Well met, Paul," said the Paul. "Hello, friend Kline."

"Cheers," said Kline.

"Just here to report," said Gous.

"Of course," said the Paul. He excused himself, went behind a desk, lifted a telephone receiver, spoke into it. A moment later he was back, unlocking the heavy door at the back of the lobby.

"Paul's expecting you," he said, holding the door wide. "Go right in."

They met the chief Paul in a room very much like the one that had been used for Kline's convalescence, the bed replaced by a sort of Victorian fainting couch, a few additional wing-backed chairs thrown in as well, the sort of room a group of nineteenth-century gentlemen would retire to after dinner to smoke their cigars. The Paul was at the piano when they came in, playing a stylized version of a song Kline knew but couldn't place. The Paul watched him, kept playing. Kline settled into one of the wing-backed chairs and listened. It was, he suddenly realized, Hank Williams' "Hey, Good Looking," reworked to sound like a German cabaret number.

When the Paul was done, Gous thumped his hand against his thigh, applauding. *What is the sound of one hand clapping?* Kline couldn't help but think. The Paul stood and gave a little bow, then came over near them, stretching out rather effetely on the fainting couch.

"Ah," he said, smiling. "Here we are again. What bliss."

Gous nodded and smiled. Kline didn't do anything.

"You are, friend Kline, I must say, a charmed man," said the Paul. "It appears you can't be killed. Though the same unfortunately cannot be said for almost anyone who comes in contact with you."

"I suppose not," said Kline.

"I see that Paul," he said, nodding at Gous, "has had to come in from the cold, so to speak. And yet I suspect, Mr. Kline, that even had he not been readily available, you would have managed to extricate yourself."

He got up and crossed to Gous, moving behind him to stand behind his wing-chair. He placed his hand and stump on Gous' head and closed his eyes. Gous too, Kline saw, had closed his eyes.

"Our father who art in all things," said the Paul sonorously, and Kline realized with surprise that this was a sort of blessing. "We ask thee, in gratitude and humility, to look kindly upon this thy servant Paul, to arrange the trees and flowers, the rocks and fields, the buildings and bodies that constitute the expression of your being here upon this earth so as to cradle him and shelter him and shield him from harm." The Paul's eyes squinted, his brow tightening. "He has gone into the mouth of affliction for thee; he has given thee not only one hand but the better part of another, more than thou doest require. Now take him into thy bosom, dear Lord, and hereafter protect him. Amen."

He lifted his hand and stump away and opened his eyes. Gous opened his eyes and looked around, as if slightly disoriented, then smiled. The Paul came back toward the fainting couch, stood in front of Kline.

"And now," he said, "Your turn, friend Kline."

"Absolutely not," said Kline.

"Why ever not, friend Kline? What could you possibly be afraid of? That you might actually feel the holy spirit?"

"None of this has anything to do with me," said Kline.

"But it could have something to do with you, friend Kline," said the Paul, regarding him steadily. "And if not, what do you have to lose? It's only a man putting his hands on your head and nothing happening at all. But what if it does have something to do with you? Wouldn't you care to know what you're missing?"

Kline let his gaze wander the room, trying to look anywhere but at Paul. He shook his head.

"Have it your way, friend Kline," said the Paul. "Nobody can be forced to believe." He sat down on the fainting couch. "And now," he said. "We've saved your life, friend Kline. The least you can do is hear us out."

"Just like Paul here," said the Paul, nodding at Gous, "I first began as part of the brotherhood. I was one of the founders, one of the first group that included, among others, Borchert and Aline, both of whom I believe you've had the pleasure of meeting. It began at first as idle speculation, an interest in certain early Christian gnostic groups followed by a fascination for certain passages of scripture, followed by the notion that indeed our hand did offend us and thus it needed to be cut off. But the leap from this conclusion to the actual physical removal of a hand itself is perhaps more difficult to explain. These were heady times, friend Kline, and had there been one less of us to spur the others on, or merely a slight shift in the atmosphere, things might well have turned out differently."

"Why are you telling me this?" asked Kline.

"Be patient, friend Kline.

"Things turned out as they were meant to turn out, and it took only the removal of the first hand—which to my eternal shame I must admit was not my own—to realize we had struck on something divine and inspired and profound." Paul stood up and paced the room, settling finally in front of the portrait of the man with his face bored away. "Before we knew it, we had begun to gather around us others, a society of men willing to go to extremes to demonstrate their faith. There were, you'll be surprised to know, Mr. Kline, more than a few. For a moment we were happy, all equals, developing a new gospel intended, through self-sacrifice, to bring ourselves closer to the divine."

"Sounds like paradise," said Kline.

Gous looked at him sharply. The Paul just turned away from the picture, smiled.

"But every paradise must end," he said. "Even a one-handed one."

"What ended this one?"

"This one?" asked the Paul. "Oh, the usual thing," he said, waving his stump.

"They went too far," said Gous.

"Yes," said the Paul. "As Paul says, they went too far. If the loss of one limb brings one closer to God, they reasoned, additional losses would bring them even closer."

"Less is more," said Gous.

"Less is more," Paul assented. He sat back down. "And everything appended thereto."

"Ramse felt that way," said Gous.

"The hierarchy, the judgment of others with fewer amputations, servitude, holier than thou. They became coarse, greedy. A real shame."

"But you didn't go along," said Kline.

"Oh, I went along," said the Paul. "At first. I had reservations but I lopped off my own foot."

"You did?" said Gous, surprised.

"It's not common knowledge as you see, friend Kline." He turned to Gous. "Just like you, Paul. I did it because I had to." He turned back to Kline. "Or you, friend Kline. I keep it covered, shoed, like you with your toes. I'm not particularly proud of it, Mr. Kline."

"And then?" said Kline.

"And then, the others kept letting more and more of themselves go. I stayed a two, and as their own amputations increased they began to separate themselves from me. Finally I gathered who I could and left."

"I'm surprised they let you leave."

"*Let* probably isn't the best word to use," Paul said. He pulled at his shirt until it came untucked, then reached across his body to tug it up. On his left side Kline saw four scarred divots, bullet wounds. "Like you, friend Kline, they didn't want me to go. Had I not already converted others to my cause I would have died in a ditch. But as it was, my comrades took me and healed me and now here we are."

"Here we are," said Kline.

"But you, Mr. Kline, made it out entirely on your own, and left them more than a little to remember you by."

"A conflagration," said Gous.

"Fire from heaven," said the Paul. "Though they themselves surely didn't see it in those terms."

"No, they didn't," said Gous.

"But we know who you are," said the Paul.

"You come not with an olive branch but with a sword," said Gous.

"You can't be killed," said the Paul. "You are the Son of God returned."

"You've got to be kidding," said Kline.

"Far from it, friend Kline," said the Paul. "We know thou art He."

"Then why don't I know?" asked Kline.

"Deep down, you know," said the Paul. "You just won't let the scales fall from your eyes."

"You're here for a purpose," said Gous.

"Yes," said the Paul.

"And what," asked Kline reluctantly, "could that purpose possibly be?"

"Mayhem," said the Paul, his voice rising. "Holy wrath. Cast down the false prophets. God wants you to destroy them. Kill them all."

Gous and Paul were close behind him, calling to him, begging him to listen. He kept moving, running as fast as he could. Doors were opening, the heads of Pauls popping out, watching him rush past.

He came to the T-intersection and went left, followed it to the second intersection, turned right, rushed down the spiral staircase, hand sliding along the heavy lacquered banister.

There was the door to the outside, the Paul he had knocked unconscious before standing in front of it.

"I'd like to leave," said Kline, breathless.

"Leave?" said the doorman Paul. "Now why, friend Kline, would you want to do that?"

"Open the door now."

"We haven't made you welcome?" asked the Paul. "Is it because you're not a Paul? I'm sorry to hear it." Lifting his hand, he turned toward the door, then paused, turned back.

"Do you have my key?"

"Your key?" asked Kline. "What do you mean?"

"To the car," said the Paul. "The one we loaned you."

"Mr. Kline," called a voice from behind him. "Surely you're not thinking of leaving us?"

He turned and there, on the stairs, a turn up, looking down, was the chief Paul, Gous beside him, dozens of Pauls clustered behind them.

"I thought I might," said Kline.

"But surely you must see, Mr. Kline, that what happened before can only happen again. They'll be waiting for you, they'll find you, and they'll kill you."

"You just said I couldn't be killed."

The Paul came down another turn, the others following. "As long as you are following God's will, friend Kline. But even God sometimes becomes impatient. You know the story of Jonah, friend Kline? How many whales do you suppose God will deign send to swallow you? When does God run out of whales?"

He came the rest of the way down until he was standing in front of Kline. "How long do you keep running, Mr. Kline? Is that really how you want to live? Listening for the sound of footsteps, heart leaping every time you see someone missing a limb? Like an animal?"

He moved a little closer, spread his arms.

"We're just trying to help you, friend."

"I don't want help," said Kline. "And I'm not your friend."

"Of course not," said the chief Paul, soothingly.

"All I want is to be left alone."

"Who could ask for anything more?" asked the Paul. "We want to leave you alone, friend Kline, we want you to come and go as you please. They're the ones who keep trying to kill you. We only want to help you."

Kline didn't say anything.

"If you'd rather not," said the chief Paul, "I can't force you. But they did remove several of your toes if I'm not mistaken, not to mention your entire arm."

"Forearm," said Kline, "and I was the one who removed it."

"Voluntarily, Mr. Kline? Or were you coerced?"

"Coerced," said Gous.

"Thank you, Paul," said the chief Paul. "'A' for effort. But I was asking our friend Kline. How can you ever live a normal life," he said, turning back to Kline, "until they're dead?"

"I'm not looking for revenge," said Kline.

"This isn't vengeance," said the chief Paul. "It's holy wrath."

Kline stared at him for a long moment and then began to pace, first in one direction then in the other, the crowd of Pauls rustling out of his way. *What sort of life do I have left for myself?* he wondered. There was still the satchel full of money, secure in a safe deposit box, assuming he could still locate the key. He could simply leave here, get the money, and vanish.

But they'd be waiting, he knew, they'd try to stop him before he could even get the money. Could he make it? Could he really vanish? Even if he did, would he still flinch every time he saw the absence of a limb?

"But of course, there's always vengeance as well," said the chief Paul, and there was a rumble from the Pauls behind him. "Wouldn't you like to kill the man who took your arm?"

"He's already dead," said Kline. "I already killed him."

"Borchert?" said Gous, and laughed. "He's far from dead."

Kline stopped moving, his missing hand tightening into a fist. "You're lying," he said.

"I assure you, he's not," said the chief Paul. "Borchert survived your little fire."

"He was dead before the fire," said Kline.

Gous shook his head. "If he was, he came back to life again," he said.

"This is a trick," Kline said, voice rising, "just to get me to kill them."

"It isn't," said the chief Paul. "Cross my heart and hope to die."

Kline started to pace again. *Curiosity is a terrible thing*, he was thinking. *How is it possible to stop oneself from needing to know?* He moved back and forth, trying to figure the best way out. Was it possible simply to walk away and disappear, to leave all this behind forever?

For him, for this, he realized, it wasn't. At least not yet.

"If I do this," said Kline. "I want never to see any of you ever again."

"Agreed," said the chief Paul.

"Even me, Mr. Kline?" asked Gous, a hurt look on his face.

"Even you, Gous," said Kline.

"Paul," said Gous.

"My point exactly," said Kline raggedly. "All right," he said, "so be it."

PART THREE

I.

What is the fewest number of them that I will have to kill? Kline wondered as he drove. *Just Borchert? Will that be enough to keep them from coming after me?*

No, he thought. At the very least he'd have to kill the guards at the gate, then three or four guards in the building. And what about the other high-level amputees? Would one of them be poised to take over from Borchert, and would he continue to hunt Kline? Would he be safe if he killed everyone with twelve amputations or more? Ten? Eight? Could he risk stopping before they were all dead?

About a mile away, he pulled the car off the road and down between some trees, out of sight from the road, then stayed there a moment, gripping the wheel, staring through the windshield at the flutter and wave of leaves in the wind. *I could turn around,* he mused. *I could drive to the police station and turn myself in,* he said, knowing even as he thought this that he wouldn't do it, that it was already too late.

He loaded the clips of each of the four pistols on the seat beside him, not easily done with one hand, then clicked them in, then affixed silencers to the end of each gun, awkwardly screwing them into place. The remainder of the bullets he placed in his jacket pockets. He placed one gun in the shoulder holster, one in the holster at his waist. The third he held in his hand. The fourth he wasn't certain what to do with, so he left it in the car.

Angel of destruction . . . he thought . . . *like a thief in the night . . . not with an olive branch but with a sword . . .*

He got out of the car and started walking, sticking close to the edge of the dirt road, always near enough to the trees that he could scramble for cover. His palm was sweating; soon, he had to put the gun down and wipe his hand dry against his shirt. When he picked the gun up again it was sticky with dust. *Hardly an auspicious beginning,* he thought.

He trudged on. Once he came in sight of the gates, he threaded his way down into the undergrowth, working slowly and carefully until he was in the last clump of bushes before open ground.

There were two guards, perhaps fifty meters away, just inside the gate.

And now what? he thought.

He stayed watching them. From time to time, one would wander in either direction down the fence and then wander back, never more than twenty or thirty meters from his companion. After a while, one guard was relieved and replaced. Kline looked at his watch. Then he waited.

The other guard was relieved two hours later.

Two hours, he thought. *In and out.*

He waited, thinking it through. He could shoot one of the guards as he wandered down the fence, but could he get back to the other and kill him before he raised the alarm? Should he wait for darkness and try to get them both at once? Where had the alarm system been? And when did they turn the lights on? He tried to remember what it had been like on his trip out, but he had been too crazed, had lost too much blood; he only remembered scattered images, he couldn't make any sense of it. One thing was as good as another, he thought; he might as well just go ahead and rush in now.

But he stayed there, waiting.

Besides, he told himself, *it doesn't matter which way I do it. I can't be killed.*

The light had started to deepen, shadows lengthening, the sun turning a dark orange and falling lower.

If I use only one clip, he told himself, *maybe I can still come out of this human.*

He balanced the gun on his knee, wiping his hand dry on his other knee. He took the gun up again. He tried to start forward, but couldn't make himself move.

Easiest thing to do was simply to lift the barrel of the gun and put it snugly into his own mouth and pull the trigger. As Frank had said, it would save everybody a lot of trouble. But then he thought of Borchert, of strangling him with his single hand and trying not to pass out. *One clip*, he told himself, *just one clip*, but realized as he thought this that he didn't care how many clips it took, nor what it might do to him.

The sun crossed the edge of the horizon and slowly went, and it was twilight. The lights hadn't yet come on, and one guard had just replaced another, and one guard was wandering out along the fence, bored, near him, and was just starting back, his back turned. Kline, crouched, came out of the bushes, and ran lightly toward him and shot him in the back of the head, the silencer giving off a dull cough as he fired. The guard went down in a heap without a sound. Kline kept running along the fence and there, at the gates, was the other guard, raising his gun prosthetic and looking at him. Kline fired and the shot, skew, struck the guard's gun arm, sparking off it. Kline fired again, the bullet this time striking the guard in the chest. The guard went down but not before a few rounds thunked out of his gun and into the dirt.

Ah, hell, thought Kline.

When he got there the man was still moving, weakly folding up, eyes glazing over in the dark, blood pumping out of his chest as he took crazed little breaths. Kline broke the man's neck with his heel, then rolled him off the roadway and between the guard box and the fence. Then he stood in front of the guard box and waited.

A few minutes later he heard the sound of steps and there, at a little distance, was a human figure, his outline clear, his features far from distinct in the darkness. Kline, his back to the guard box, hoped he was even less distinct, that the gun would look enough like a gun-arm to pass.

"Everything okay?" the figure asked.

"Everything okay," Kline said.

"What about the shots?"

"That wasn't from here," said Kline.

"No? Where's your partner?"

"Down the fence a little way," said Kline. "He went to see if there's a problem."

"That's not procedure," said the man.

"I told him not to do it."

The man cursed softly, then sighed. And then, a different note entering his voice, he asked, "Why haven't you turned on the lights?"

Kline quickly shot him, aiming for his head. The man disappeared into the darkness of the ground and Kline could hear him thrashing loudly, gurgling. Kline rushed forward and fell on him and struck him on the head with the pistol, then dropped the pistol and strangled him with one hand, the guard's eyes vague glints in the darkness that slowly went away.

The guard's neck was wet and slippery, and to strangle him properly Kline had to block the hole he had shot in his throat. By the time he pulled his arm away it was slippery and wet with blood, and he had to wipe his hand as best he could on the dead man's pants before groping the gun out of the darkness and getting up.

Three dead, he thought. *But four bullets. But still human.*

He started along the road, keeping to one side of it. Ahead were a few lights, the heart of the compound.

Two bullets left, he thought, and then wished he'd thought to ask for a Browning.

He passed a row of houses, light coming out of most of them, then turned down a smaller road, keeping to one side, houses a little more spread out now. He entered a third, smaller, tree-lined alley that dead-ended in front of the small two-story building he had briefly lived in.

From there, he backtracked, searched around until he found the path cutting away from the road, its crushed white shells luminous and unearthly in the darkness. He followed the path carefully, keeping to one side of it to avoid crunching the shells beneath his feet.

The path moved into the trees, then dipped down. There was, he remembered suddenly, a security camera somewhere, affixed to a tree, and then he wondered how many cameras he had already passed without noticing. *Did they broadcast to the guard box by the gate*, he wondered, *or to somewhere else?* He should have gone inside the guard box, at least looked, but it was too late now.

There it was, an angular irregularity high on the shadow of one of the trees. He pushed his way through the brush and back into the trees and around the camera, slowly working his way back to the path, which turned out to be difficult, because the path had curved away. He followed the path uphill where it widened into a tree-lined avenue.

There, in front of him and behind its fence, was the old manor house, some of its windows lit and casting a gentle glow on the lawn. There was still, Kline noticed, the smell of burning in the air. It grew stronger as, crouching, he came closer. The lawn was darker in spots and probably burnt away, streaks of smoke all up one side of the building. Looking through the fence he saw, near the entrance, a pile of lumber, a bandsaw. *At least*, he thought, *I made an impression.*

What now? he wondered, and started searching for the guard. There he was, just inside the fence, there near the gate. *What now?* he wondered.

He stood up and moved rapidly toward the gate.

"Don't shoot," he said. "Don't shoot. It's me, Ramse."

"Ramse," said the guard. "What—" and by that time Kline was close enough to shoot him in the head.

Only the guard didn't go down. He seemed instead like he'd been switched off. He just stood there unmoving, his empty eye socket open, the side of his head torn away and oozing. Kline lifted the gun again, but the guard didn't even respond. He slowly lowered the gun, then helped the guard first to sit then lie down. He left him there, staring into the sky.

One bullet left, he thought. *Still human.*

Mostly, he thought, and moved toward the door.

He knocked, and the door opened slightly.

"What is wanted?" asked the guard, and then saw Kline's face. He tried to close the door, but Kline already had the barrel of the pistol wedged in the crack and shot him in the chest. The guard fell back, gasping, trying to raise his gun prosthesis, but Kline was already through the doorway and on top of him, forcing the man's arm to fold the gun prosthesis back so that when it went off it fired into the guard's belly and was muffled between their two bodies.

Kline held still and listened, keeping his hand over the guard's mouth as the man slowly died beneath him. The shots, despite being muffled, still echoed down the hall, or so it seemed to Kline, right on top of the gun.

He waited, but nothing happened. *How is it possible,* he thought, *that nobody heard?* He rolled slowly off the guard and lay beside him, gathering his breath. He was soaked with blood now, wet with it from neck to knees. The guard beside him was even bloodier, though his face was pale as porcelain, expressionless as a plate. Kline sat up.

Out of bullets, he thought and dropped the pistol. He reached for the gun holstered at his waist and then hesitated, picking the first gun off the floor. He ejected the clip, reloaded it.

Six bullets left, he told himself. *Still human.*

I've beat the system, he thought, and then thought, *no.* This was simply a sign that he'd already stopped being human and wasn't planning on coming back.

How was it that they had done it? he tried to remember, staring at the end of the white hall. *Two times? Three times?*

Three, he thought it was. He knocked three times and waited. Nothing happened. He tried it again and heard movement on the other side, and a moment later the door opened and a guard pushed his face out, his single eye puffy with sleep, and Kline shot him dead.

How many does that make? Kline wondered idly, and then was amazed that he didn't immediately know. He shoved at the door until he'd slid the dead guard forward enough that he could squeeze his way in and step over him and into the stairwell. Slowly he started up, only beginning to become aware of the smell that the blood he was covered with seemed to have. It reminded him of something, but he couldn't place it. *What if the Pauls are right?* he couldn't help but wonder. He tried not to think about it.

He stopped at the third and final landing. Very carefully he opened the door a crack, half-expecting to see a dozen guards there waiting for him, but he saw nobody. *I can't be killed,* thought Kline, and then thought, *I'm slowly going mad.*

No, he thought, as he opened the door wide and stepped into the hall, *quickly.*

He made his way to the door at the end of the hall, pressing his ear to it. There was a sound from the other side, a low and constant humming, and occasionally something rising above it.

He pushed at the door's lever with his elbow, found it unlocked. Slowly he pushed it the rest of the way down, opened the door, slipped quietly in.

It was different inside from when he had last been there. The walls were in the process of being redone, covered with sheetrock that wasn't yet taped or painted. The varnish of the floor, especially near the door, was blistered and scorched. Borchert's simple pallet had been replaced by a hospital bed, identical to the one Kline himself had occupied. The humming was coming from a machine beside the bed, from which a tube ran, connecting to a breathing mask covering Borchert's mouth and nose. He was lying in the bed, swathed in gauze. What Kline could see of his skin was red and peeling and puckered, his hair all gone save for a ragged, ravaged clump. Beside him, sitting in a wheelchair, her back toward Kline, was a legless nurse in a starched white uniform, her back very straight, in the process of replacing the dressings around Borchert's foot.

Kline moved slowly forward. The nurse, still working on the foot, chatting idly, didn't hear him. But Borchert cocked his head.

"Who is it?" he said, into the mask, his breath fogging the plastic. His voice was flatter than normal, Kline noticed, not quite Borchert's voice, something seriously wrong with it. It was, he realized, the voice he'd heard on the telephone in the hospital.

"There's no one," the nurse was saying. "It's just me."

Borchert opened his eyes and Kline saw that it was opaque and dull, seemingly without pupil. Blind. He took another step forward.

"There's someone here," said Borchert. "I can feel it."

The nurse turned slightly and caught sight of Kline out of the corner of her eye, froze. Kline pointed the gun at her.

"You're right," she said.

"Who is it?" Borchert asked.

"It's him," said the nurse.

They stayed like that for a moment then the nurse turned back, finished winding the dressing. Kline came quickly behind her and struck her hard on the head with the pistol butt. She slumped, the top half of her collapsing onto Borchert. Borchert winced. Kline dragged her back into the wheelchair, wheeled her to face against the wall, where he could see her, and set the brakes.

"So we haven't managed to kill you after all, Mr. Kline," said Borchert. "Not, I must say, for lack of trying. You seem to live a charmed life."

"What happened to your eye?" asked Kline.

Borchert smiled, the movement distorting his face terribly. "Always wanting to know, Mr. Kline. You'd think you'd have learned your lesson. Did you come here just to ask me that?"

"Not exactly," said Kline.

"Not exactly," said Borchert. "Always holding something back, Mr. Kline. Intimacy issues, perhaps?" And he smiled wider, the damaged skin just beside his mouth cracking, growing moist with a pinkish fluid in the cracks, leaking.

"What did you do with the girl?" asked Borchert. "Kill her?"

"No," said Kline. "Unconscious."

"Ah," said Borchert. "Still pretending to be human, are we?" Kline watched his smile tighten further, then slowly die. "Where were we?" he asked.

"Your eye," said Kline.

"I thought we'd sidled our way past that," said Borchert. "What happened to my eye, Mr. Kline, was you. You are also what happened to my face, my body, my voice. And now I imagine you've come to finish the job."

"Yes," said Kline.

"I don't suppose you could be convinced to give this one a pass?"

"I don't suppose so," said Kline.

"Say I call off the hunt, Mr. Kline? Say I solemnly swear not to pursue you, grant you immunity as it were?"

Kline hesitated.

"No," he said finally. "I can't trust you."

"I hear the hesitation in your voice, Mr. Kline. Why not give in to it?"

Should I? he wondered. And then he thought of each of the men he had killed, seven, unless it was eight, unless it was nine, the way they had each fallen. What did he owe them, now that he was here? *Owe them?* he thought. No, that was just him pretending to be human again. He didn't owe them anything. But they were a part of a velocity that still carried him forward and he didn't know how to stop without killing Borchert.

"Well, Mr. Kline?" said Borchert. "How about it?"

But then Kline caught out of the corner of his eye the nurse, still pretending to be unconscious, slowly lifting something out of the seat of her wheelchair, and he realized with a start that it was a gun. As she suddenly came alive and tried to turn it toward him he shot her twice in the head.

Borchert sighed in the bed. "I see you found her gun. Worth a try," he said. And then said, still inflectionless, "Hardly gentlemanly to shoot a lady. You could have simply disarmed her, Mr. Kline. What's happening to you?"

What indeed? wondered Kline.

"Well," said Borchert, "what are we waiting for? Get it over with."

"Not quite yet," said Kline.

"Not yet?" said Borchert.

"First," said Kline, "there are a few things I want to know."

Borchert smiled again, this time so wide Kline thought fleetingly his face was coming asunder. "Ah, Mr. Kline," he said. "We never seem to learn, do we."

◆◆◆

"Shall we say twenty questions, Mr. Kline?"

"What?" said Kline.

"Nineteen questions then?" said Borchert. "And then you can kill me?"

"Suits me," said Kline.

"Always game for a game, Mr. Kline? But what am I to receive for my cooperation? Perhaps my life?"

"No," said Kline.

"Not my life? Then what, Mr. Kline? What's my so-called motivation?"

"Your motivation?"

"Eighteen," said Borchert. "You should be more careful. Simply this: Why should I answer your questions? I'm dead either way."

"True," said Kline.

"Perhaps . . ." said Borchert. "It's not much, but perhaps I might be allowed to choose the manner of my own death?"

The nurse, Kline noticed, was apparently still alive, her hand quivering against the floor and sending ripples through the pooling blood. He went over to her, prodded her with his foot, turned her face up. She seemed dead, except for her eye, which, unblinking, followed each of his movements.

"Well, Mr. Kline?"

"What about paralysis?" asked Kline.

"Excuse me?" said Borchert. "Seventeen."

He moved his hand slowly, the gun in it, watched her eye follow it. Was there any sign of intelligence in the eye's movement? In the eye itself? Was she still human? More human than he?

"Have I lost you, Mr. Kline?"

"No," said Kline. "I'm right here."

"What are you doing over there?"

"Nothing," said Kline, watching the nurse's eye. "What about paralysis? Does it count the same as amputation?"

"Sixteen and fifteen, Mr. Kline. Is it religious instruction you're hoping for? Paralysis is a shadow and a type of amputation, a next best thing. We do not accept paralytics among us, but we look kindly on them. You have to draw the line somewhere, Mr. Kline."

"I see," said Kline. He watched the eye until he couldn't bear it anymore and then struck her hard on the forehead with the pistol.

Immediately the pupil rolled back and was gone.

"But we have yet to reach an agreement, Mr. Kline, and you've already expended a quarter of your questions. I must ask again: Will I be allowed to choose the manner of my own death?"

"Within reason," said Kline, turning back toward him.

"Something quickly achieved, within this room, no tricks? Can we agree to that?"

"What is it?"

"Fourteen," said Borchert. "There's that curiosity again, Mr. Kline. Shall we say I'll tell you at the end? Once you've had your other answers?"

Kline thought. "All right," he finally said.

"Fine," said Borchert, "just fine. What would you like to know?"

"Tell me about Paul," said Kline.

"That's not a question," said Borchert. "Shall we rephrase it as *Will you please tell me about Paul?* Thirteen." He smiled again. "Ah, Paul," he said. "I knew he was behind this. Paul used to number himself among the faithful, Mr. Kline. Now he numbers himself among the fallen."

"What is he like?"

"Twelve," said Borchert.

"That shouldn't count as twelve," said Kline. "It's the same question."

"It's a modification of the original question," said Borchert, "*ergo,* no longer the same question. Twelve." Borchert stretched slightly. A plate of pink skin under one arm split, began to suppurate a yellowish substance. "Paul likes exactness and order. He wants everything to be the same. He's a great believer in the saving power of art and culture and, perhaps as a consequence, of the saving gestures of ritual. He's into the ritual of the worship—relics, ceremonies."

"Can I trust him?"

Borchert gave a barking laugh. "You should know better than to ask a question like that. Particularly of me. Who's to say if anyone can be trusted, Mr. Kline? Eleven."

"When I kill you, what will they do?"

"They Pauls or they us?"

"Both."

"That's two questions, Mr. Kline. Ten, nine. What we'll do is convene and decide on a new leader. What they'll do is rejoice at my death. I'm sure they have plans for you."

"What sort of plans?"

"Let's suspend that question for now," said Borchert. "Let's work our way toward that one."

"Who will take your place?"

"Eight. Our process is very simple, Mr. Kline. They'll opt for the person with the most amputations. In case of same number of amputations, one must rely on charisma and Godly vision. It could be either of two men whose rooms are to be found on this floor, at this end of the hall."

"And after them?"

"After them, Mr. Kline? One of the three other men on this floor. Seven."

"And after that?"

"Six. Not very original questions, Mr. Kline. You don't know how to play properly. After that, the next floor down. And then, after that, the ground floor. Then outside and to the nines, among which probably chief among them would be your former associate, Mr. Ramse."

"I thought he was an eight," said Kline.

"He indeed was an eight," said Borchert. "But now he's a nine. Five."

"It wasn't a question," said Kline. "It was a statement."

"It was fishing for information," said Borchert. "Thus a question. 'Isn't he an eight?' you might as well have said."

"Where does Ramse live?"

"Excuse me?"

"Where does Ramse live?"

Borchert paused, hesitated. "I wish I could see your face, Mr. Kline. I'd like to know exactly what you hope to gain from this question. Don't suppose you care to tell me?"

"His address," said Kline.

"Perhaps we should suspend this," said Borchert. "Just gently call a stop to it and allow you to kill me in whatever manner you please."

"If you'd like," said Kline.

"I don't like giving out information whose use strikes me as uncertain."

"Perhaps I just want to see an old friend."

"Not likely, Mr. Kline. But then again, what does it matter to me once I'm dead?"

"That's the spirit," said Kline.

"And there's always the matter of choosing my own death."

"Within reason," said Kline.

"Yes," said Borchert. "Exactness and order in all things. I'm aware of the terms," he said, and told him how to find Ramse's house. "Three more, Mr. Kline," he said, once he was done.

Kline nodded, but of course Borchert couldn't see. The gun had grown sweaty in his hand. He stuck it into his jacket pocket, rubbed his hand against his pants. The hand came back sticky with blood.

"How many of you do I have to kill before you'll leave me alone?" asked Kline.

"How many?" said Borchert, and smiled. "Don't you realize you'll have to kill all of us, Mr. Kline?" he said. "Every last one."

"Two more questions, Mr. Kline," said Borchert. "Do you feel like you've gained something? What do you do with all this knowledge of yours? Do you feel more complete?"

Kline didn't say anything.

"Well, then," said Borchert. "Your move, Mr. Kline."

"What sort of plans do the Pauls have for me?"

"Ah, yes," said Borchert. "The return of the repressed. Isn't it obvious, Mr. Kline?"

"No," said Kline.

Borchert pursed his lips. "Try harder, Mr. Kline," he said. "Consider Paul. A young man who likes things in their place, a strong believer in ritual and in some of the traditions of the old church—the so-called relics of his so-called saints for instance." He smiled. "We have our spies too, Mr. Kline. We know the Pauls inside and out. Think, Mr. Kline, what would a man like that want with you?"

"I don't know," said Kline.

"You do know, Mr. Kline. Think. He thinks of you as their messiah. But messiahs' lives are always messy. What can one do with a messiah so as to allow Him to enter unsullied into the realm of myth?"

"I don't know."

"Martyr Him, of course. Crucify Him."

Kline felt his limbs grow suddenly heavy, the missing limb most of all. Borchert was making a repeated barking sound, like he was choking to death, his breathing mask fogging inside. It took Kline some time to realize he was laughing.

"You're lying," said Kline. "It was you who wanted to crucify me."

Borchert stopped barking. "Of course we wanted to crucify you," he said, "but as one of the two thieves. It's different for them. Think it through, Mr. Kline."

Kline stayed motionless, watching Borchert's damaged face twitch.

"Why?" he finally asked.

"Why?" asked Borchert, and his whole body seemed to flinch. "Because Paul believes in you, Mr. Kline. Paul thinks you're the one. You came like a thief in the night. You came bearing not an olive branch but a sword. You left a swath of fire and destruction in your path. You seem to him as if you are impossible to slay by mortal means. In his eyes, you are the Son of Man, which is to say the Son of God."

"I'm not," said Kline.

"And what does one do with the Son of Man?" asked Borchert. "One crucifies Him, of course. One does him the favor of helping Him step out of this mortal round, thus making the Son of Man the Son of God. There's also of course the matter of you being the only person among the Pauls more powerful than he. At this point, Mr. Kline, you're more useful to him dead than alive."

"What should I do?"

"Alas, Mr. Kline, you've run out of questions. You'll have to figure that one out on your own. Or rather you have one more question that awaits an answer: *How does Mr. Borchert choose to die?*"

"How does Mr. Borchert choose to die?" asked Kline.

"In the back," said Borchert, "near the hotplate, you'll find a cleaver. I believe you're already rather familiar with its mode of operation. I want you to deliver one final amputation. I want you to separate my head from my body."

"You what?"

"You promised," said Borchert. "A dying man's final request."

Kline didn't say anything.

"It's not that I believe in you exactly," said Borchert. "But I wouldn't say I don't believe in you either. Let's just say I'm hedging my bets."

And then it came again, that barking laugh.

There's no reason to do it, part of him kept saying as he went to fetch the cleaver. *Just shoot him in the head and be done with him.* But another part of him was saying, *Why not? What did it matter?* He had come here with the intention of killing Borchert: why not kill him in this way?

And a third part of himself, the part that terrified him the most, was saying, *What if Paul is right? What if I am God?*

There will always be three of me from now on, he thought, or a third part of him thought, or a fourth part of him thought, and he shook his head.

He was back at the bed, holding the cleaver now, staring down at Borchert.

"Ready?" he asked.

"Go ahead," said Borchert, and Kline felt his hand raise the cleaver and then bring it down hard.

A neck, it turned out, was not nearly so easy as an elbow. Either that or the cleaver was duller than it had been, or Kline flinched when he delivered the blow, or it was not a clean blow to begin with. Or it was simply the fact that Borchert's neck, when compressed, was slightly wider than the cleaver's blade. It took a second blow, Borchert's mouth contorted already into a rictus, and then a third, but even once the spine was severed there was still a thick band of intact flesh, and finally he had to post his stump against Borchert's chin and push the head away from the neck so that the band of flesh grew taut and could be cut. Borchert's eyelids fluttered, fell still. There was blood everywhere.

He went to the door and tried to open it only to realize he was still holding the cleaver. He felt he had lived all this already, and dropped the cleaver. His guns too he took out, all three of them, and let them fall to the floor.

He started out into the hallway, found it deserted, and then had second thoughts and went back in. Gathering the cleaver, he slipped it into his belt. Borchert's head too he gathered, holding it by its sole clump of hair. And then he started out again.

II.

How do you know the moment when you cease to be human? Is it the moment when you decide to carry a head before you by its hair, extended before you like a lantern, as if you are Diogenes in search of one just man? Or is it the moment where reality, previously a smooth surface one slides one's way along, begins to come in waves, for a moment altogether too much and then utterly absent? Or is it the moment when you begin opening doors, showing each man behind each door the head of his spiritual leader before killing him with the cleaver tucked into your belt? Or is it the moment when all these dead begin to talk to you in a dull, rumbling murmur? Or is it the moment when these same voices suddenly fade away and stop talking altogether, leaving you utterly alone?

I am remarkably calm, thought Kline, moving from room to room. *I am doing remarkably well*, he thought, *considering.*

Or was it the moment, one floor down, when he opened a door and saw a man missing various digits and limbs, a ten or an eleven, and showed him Borchert's head and then, instead of killing the man right away, spent some time positioning Borchert's head on the floor so that it was looking at the man, so that it would have to see what came next? That next being Kline groping the cleaver out of his belt and advancing forward with the cleaver raised as the man began to give hoarse cries and beg inarticulately for mercy.

◆ ◆ ◆

By the time he opened the last door on the bottom floor of the building, by the time he had killed several dozen mutilates with the cleaver, he was figuring out ways to pretend to be human again. He was thinking of the money in the briefcase, what he might do with it once everyone else in the world was dead. He was thinking of Paul, of the Pauls, wondering whether Borchert had been right after all. He was considering what he would have to do next. Beneath these thoughts he could feel the writhing motion of the limbs and torsos and heads trying to scuttle away from him—here, the rising of a bloody head, there the shock and rapid seep of an open and fresh wound filling with blood, a bluish-white fist of bone torn from its socket, the reduction of bodies to spongy meat and slicks of blood and shattered, drying bone. *How many?* he wondered, and found himself unable to count them out, nor even quite able to grasp how he had moved from room to room: left with little beyond the act of positioning Borchert's head and then lifting the cleaver high, all of it starting to overlap with the other instances when he had raised a cleaver and brought it down upon himself. And this, indeed, was the most terrible thing of all: each blow he sunk into an arm or a leg or a chest or a head—each of these blows in any case which he could remember—he had felt going into his own body as well.

"Almost over," he said to Borchert's head, "almost done," and then wondered idly when the head would start to talk back.

He opened the front door. It was still dark outside, the night cloudless and with no moon, the stars bright. The guard was still there, his body lying beside the fence, still motionless but breathing, still staring into the air. Kline stepped gingerly around him.

He followed the path back to the rest of the complex, moving cautiously until he was among the larger houses. Once he nearly crossed paths with a guard and was forced to press himself between some bushes and a house's wall until the man had passed. But quickly he was following Borchert's directions again, and soon was standing outside Ramse's door.

He tried the door and found it locked. There was a stained glass panel on the top portion of the door and he broke it out with Borchert's head, sweeping the glass off the casement with the side of Borchert's face. He pushed the head in and heard it thump softly on the floor. He managed to steady himself on the edge of the doorframe enough to get one foot up and onto the doorhandle, and then grabbed the edge of the broken panel and pulled himself up, and then reached in deep through the panel and managed to unlock the door. A moment later he was inside.

He turned on the bedside lamp then stood beside the bed, watching Ramse sleep. He seemed peaceful, serene, his face as pale and motionless as if made of wax. It was almost a shame to wake him.

He balanced Borchert's head on the nightstand, facing away from the bed. Tugging the cleaver from his belt, he sat down on the edge of the mattress.

"Ramse," he said, "Wake up."

Ramse's face scrunched, going from wax to flesh then back again. His eyes fluttered a little then opened, remaining unfocused but slowly coming together on Kline's face. At first they just stared, and then a dull sluggish fear began to build behind them.

"It's all right, Ramse," said Kline. "It's me, Kline." *More or less*, he thought.

"That's what I'm afraid of," said Ramse, voice still hoarse with sleep.

"No reason to be afraid," said Kline.

"What happened to you?" asked Ramse. "Are you dead?"

Kline looked down, saw his blood-soaked chest. "Nothing happened to me," he said. "I'm what happened to them."

"What's that supposed to mean?" asked Ramse, voice rising, and Kline gestured to the bedside table.

"There's part of it," Kline said.

Ramse turned and saw the back of Borchert's head. He tried to speak but it came out in a shriek. Kline lifted his cleaver and shook his head and Ramse stopped. He looked back to the head, swallowed hard.

"Is it Gous?" he said, and looked like he was going to cry.

"Of course not," said Kline. "It's Borchert."

"I don't believe you," said Ramse.

Kline sighed. He put the cleaver down on the bed, reached over to turn the head to face Ramse.

"Believe me now?" he asked.

Ramse just nodded.

"I just wanted to make you *au courant*," said Kline. "To summarize: I slaughtered the guards at the gate. Then I killed everyone in the stone building that Borchert is in. Or rather was in. Which makes you next to run things, no?"

"Me or DeNardo," said Ramse. "Are you planning to kill us?"

"I don't want to kill you," said Kline. "DeNardo's a nine too?"

Ramse nodded.

"Only two nines?"

"No," said Ramse. "There are four of us. The other two won't be chosen."

"Why not?"

"It's complicated," said Ramse. He was starting to calm down a little. "Let's just say one isn't interested, the other has made too many enemies."

"Should I kill DeNardo?"

"What?" asked Ramse.

"Are you certain you can beat him?"

"Almost certain."

"You have to be certain," said Kline.

He watched Ramse think, turning it slowly over in his head.

"I can leave Borchert's head with you if you think that'll help," said Kline.

Ramse, looking terrified, shook his own head. "It wouldn't help," he said.

"Fine," Kline said. "Borchert is coming with me then."

"I'm certain," Ramse finally said.

"All right," said Kline. "Good. Now listen very carefully," he said. "If I'm to let you live, I need a promise from you."

"What is it?"

"I want to be left alone," said Kline. "I never want to see any of you ever again."

"Of course I'm going to say yes," said Ramse. "But how can you believe me?"

"Look around you, Ramse," said Kline. "Go outside and look and tally up the number of the dead. And then think about how many there are and about the fact that none of them are me. The only thing they all wanted was for me to be dead and I'm the only one of them still alive."

Ramse swallowed, nodded.

"Wouldn't you rather have a truce?"

"Again," said Ramse, using his stumps to push himself a little higher in the bed, "how can I say anything but yes?"

Kline smiled thinly, feeling the dried blood around his mouth crack. "There's always Gous," he said.

"What about Gous?" said Ramse.

"You break your promise and I'll kill Gous. I'll send him to you bit by bit."

"What do I care about Gous?" asked Ramse.

"You had a falling out," said Kline. "But what's a little thing like religion between old friends? Besides, he's coming back into the fold."

"He told you that?"

"He doesn't know it yet," said Kline. "But he will."

"How would you know? What are you, some kind of prophet?" asked Ramse.

"I'm beginning to wonder," said Kline. "Now which is it?" he asked. "Truce or war?"

Ramse stared at him for a long moment. "Truce," he finally said, and stuck out his stump.

"Good enough for me," Kline said, touching it with his own stump. Sticking the cleaver back in his belt and taking the head by its remaining hair, he made for the door.

III.

At a little distance was a guard, strolling casually, but Kline faded into shadow and let the man live. He approached the gate slowly but it was still as deserted as it had been when he'd left it, the dead still comfortably dead in the places they had fallen. Hadn't it been two hours since he had gone in? he wondered, and then wondered if this was a trap. He walked out with his neck prickling, waiting for the shots to come.

But they didn't come. He walked slowly and carefully out the gate without any trouble and then made his way down the road, weary now. He dumped the bullets from his pockets into the dust of the road, letting them go one by one. He passed where he had hidden his car at first, but then backtracked and found it, threw the head in, got in, drove.

He stopped at a closed gas station with a payphone at one end of its lot. The ashtray of the car was crammed with loose change and he took all of it with him. Calling the operator, he mentioned a town, asked to be connected to the police station.

"Second precinct," said a voice.

"I'm looking for Frank," he said.

"Frank who?" the voice asked.

"The detective," he said. "He told me to call," Kline said. "It's regarding those mutilates."

"*That* Frank," said the officer, "Frank Metterspahr. He's still in the hospital. Why don't you tell me about it?"

"Has to be Frank," Kline said. "I'll call back," he said, and hung up the telephone.

He immediately dialed the operator again, gave the name of the town again, asked to be connected to the hospital.

"Which hospital?" she asked.

"The biggest one," he said, and then waited impatiently to be connected.

When they answered he claimed he was a florist, that he was at the other hospital across town with a heap of flowers for someone named Frank. Matterball or something like that, couldn't quite read the card. Had he gone to the wrong hospital?

"Yes," she said. "He's right here, intensive care, fifth floor. But isn't it a little early to be delivering flowers?"

Well, yes, he admitted, and looked out the phone booth and at the sky caught somewhere between night and morning. But there were a lot of deliveries today and generally they'd just leave them at the desk to be taken up later, would that be all right?

He had hung up the telephone and was on the way back to the car, when it began to ring again. He looked at it awhile, then went back to answer it.

"You're the guy called earlier?" said the voice. "Looking for Frank? I'm the officer who talked to you?"

"Yes," Kline said. "That was me."

"I just talked to Frank," the man said. "He said to tell you to tell me whatever you know."

"Only to Frank," Kline said.

"All right," the man said smoothly. "That's okay too. Why don't you stay there and we'll come get you and take you to him?"

What would an informer do? he wondered.

"Frank promised me money," he finally said. "Two hundred dollars."

"Fine," said the officer. "We'll back up whatever Frank promised."

"All right," he said. "I guess that's all right."

"So stay there and we'll come get you," said the officer.

"You'll bring the money?"

"Yes," the officer said.

"All right," he said. "I'll be right here. I'll be waiting."

Hanging up the telephone he got into the car and drove away as quickly as he could.

◆◆◆

He managed to force a service door with the blade of the cleaver, the gap between metal door and metal frame being too big, and made his way up a back stairwell. An alarm started when he opened the door but immediately stopped again when he closed it. He hurried quickly upward.

The door to the fifth floor was unlocked. He put Borchert's head down and slowly cracked the door open, saw a deserted hall, every other light extinguished. There was, at the far end of the hall, a nurse's station, the nurse asleep but sitting up, nodded off.

Propping the door open with his foot, he picked the head back up, made his way in.

He went into the first room he saw, found it to contain two beds, both empty. The next one contained an older lady, asleep or unconscious, her bed lamp still on, a tube snaked down her throat, flakes of blood in her hair. He went out. The nurse at the desk was awake now, but not looking his way.

He slipped across the hall and into a third room, found both curtains drawn. He opened one, found a man, his hands strapped down, his head covered in bandages that blood had seeped through, unless it was mere shadow. The man's eyes were the only thing moving, rolling madly in his sockets and then suddenly focusing sharply on Kline. The man made a strange muffled sound and shifted his head slightly and Kline saw that yes, it was not just shadow, but blood. He pulled the curtain closed.

Behind the second curtain was Frank, asleep. One arm was out on top of the blankets, the other was missing, amputated between the elbow and the shoulder, dressed and wrapped. Kline scooted a chair toward the bed. With his foot he pulled the curtain closed. Holding Borchert's head in his lap, he waited for Frank to wake up.

After a while he realized that something wasn't quite right. Frank was too still. Fleetingly he thought Frank was dead, but no, he was breathing. And then he realized what it must be.

He reached out, prodded Frank's dressings with a finger.

"I can tell you're not asleep," he said.

"Never claimed to be," said Frank, his eyes slitting open.

Kline smiled. They both stared at one another.

"Why are you here?" asked Frank finally. "To kill me?"

"I want to turn myself in," said Kline.

Frank laughed. "This isn't a police station," he said. "Why come here?"

"I thought I owed it to you," said Kline.

"What exactly do you want to turn yourself in about?" asked Frank.

"This," said Kline, and lifted up Borchert's head.

"Good God," said Frank. "What the hell did you bring that in here for?"

"Evidence," said Kline.

"I don't particularly want to see it," said Frank. "Why don't you put it on the nightstand?" he said. "Or, better yet, on the floor."

Kline put Borchert's head on the floor, against the bed's leg.

"What was that exactly?" asked Frank.

"Borchert," said Kline. "Leader of the mutilates."

"He owes me an arm," said Frank. "I'm glad he's dead."

"He's not the only dead," said Kline.

"Who else?"

"I don't know."

"You don't know?"

"Not names," said Kline. "A few dozen people. More or less. I killed them."

"Mutilates?"

Kline nodded.

"How many left?"

"I don't know."

"Jesus Christ," said Frank. "Talk about an avenging angel. And now you've decided to turn yourself in?"

"That's right," said Kline.

"Why?"

"So I can be human again."

"Buddy," said Frank. "Look at yourself. You're covered head to toe in blood. You're never going to be human again."

Kline looked away. He looked at the head on the floor. When he looked back, Frank was still staring at him.

"So now what?" Kline said.

"Now what? You want to turn yourself in, go down to the police station and do it. Don't come around here with your bag full of heads expecting me to do something about it. What do you want? Sympathy? Understanding? Hell if I'll be part of it."

"I only have one head," said Kline.

"Last I saw you had two," said Frank, "the one you're wearing and the one you're carrying. That's one head too many. Maybe in your case two too many. How the hell is it you're not dead?"

Kline shrugged.

"That's it?" said Frank. "You come in carrying a head and say there are a few dozen more where that came from and when I ask you how it is you're still alive all you can do is shrug?"

"Just lucky, I guess," said Kline.

"Lucky?" said Frank. "Blessed is more like it."

"Don't say that," said Kline.

"What do you want me to say?"

Kline shook his head.

"All right," said Frank. "You've had a hard day, with the multiple killings and all. I'll cut you some slack. One question though."

"What?"

"Why are you still here? Why can't you get out and leave me in peace?"

IV.

It was morning by the time he got to his apartment. He rang the super's bell and the super buzzed the front door open, but upon seeing Kline, bloody and carrying the cleaver, he tried to close the door to his apartment. Kline was too quick. He knocked him down as the man babbled. He tried to tie him up, finding it too difficult to do well with a single hand, finally knocking him out with the flat of the cleaver and locking him inside a closet.

The keys to his apartment were on one of a series of hooks in the kitchen, just above the sink. He tore the cords for both of the super's phones out of the wall, then left, climbing the stairs to his apartment.

When he got there he found the door ajar, the police tape across it broken.

Does it never stop? he wondered.

He pushed the door open slowly and, cleaver held ready, went in. The air was dusty and thick. He could see in the dim light from the hallway the dust on the floor, dust that he was now stirring up in slow, drunken eddies. There were other footprints, he saw, dim tracks covered over with dust, smears too on the floor and beneath this the glints of broken glass like dim eyes, and a dark spread of dried blood. And also another pair of footprints, singular, newer, dustless, leading him forward.

The footprints led him out of the entrance hall and back into the apartment. There, in the bedroom, was Gous. He didn't notice Kline at first, just kept sitting and staring idly at his mutilated hand, tracing the smooth flesh from his third finger down to his wrist, stroking it like it was an animal.

"Are you alone?" Kline finally asked quietly.

Gous jumped. "Oh," he said, when he saw Kline. "It's you."

"You didn't answer the question," said Kline.

"Yes," said Gous. "Alone. Just me, Paul."

"What are you doing here?"

"I came to get you," said Gous. "Paul wants to see you. He wants you to report."

"Which Paul?" said Kline. "And what do you mean, report?"

"The first Paul," said Gous. "He wants to know how it went."

Kline came a step further into the room, putting the cleaver down on the edge of the bed. Gous' eyes flicked to it and flicked quickly back, and for just a moment Kline thought maybe he himself had finally made a mistake. But Gous made no move for it.

"I'm going to take a shower," said Kline, and stripped off his shirt.

"Don't you want to report?"

"No," said Kline.

"No?"

"I'll tell you about it and then you can go tell Paul."

Gous shook his head. "Paul insisted you come in person."

"No," said Kline. "I won't come."

"Why?"

"Because Paul wants to kill me."

Gous laughed. "Why would Paul want to kill you?"

"We had a deal," said Kline. "I kept my half of it. His half was that I never had to see any of the Pauls ever again."

"Even me?" asked Gous.

"Even you," said Kline. "Even though you're not really a Paul."

"Don't say that," said Gous, giving him a pained look. He stood up, sighed. "Paul said you might prove difficult," he said. He took a gun out of his pocket and, gripping it awkwardly, pointed it at Kline. "I'm going to have to insist," he said.

Does it never stop? thought Kline again.

"You know what he wants to do to me, Gous?" he asked.

"He wants to talk to you," said Gous.

"He wants to kill me," said Kline. "He wants to crucify me."

The gun wavered slightly in Gous' hand, then steadied again. Kline inched forward. "It isn't true," Gous said.

"It is," said Kline. "Do you want me dead?"

"Not particularly," said Gous.

"I didn't kill Ramse," said Kline, and watched the gun waver again, go steady.

"No?" said Gous.

"No," said Kline.

"I suppose that's good," said Gous. "I don't like to imagine him dead."

"If you take me back," said Kline, "they'll kill me."

"No," said Gous. "We won't."

"Then why the gun? Why would Paul insist on me reporting in person? Why would that matter?"

Gous shrugged. "How should I know?"

Kline sighed. "All right," he said. "What else can I do?" he asked. He started to turn away and then half-turned back. "One other thing," he said. "That gun won't do you any good."

"Why not?" asked Gous.

"Haven't you heard?" said Kline. "I can't be killed." And this time when the gun wavered, Kline's hand was already on it, tearing it out of Gous' grasp.

He made Gous turn around and raise his hand and then struck him on the back of the head with the butt of the pistol. He left him lying there in a heap on the floor while he slipped out of his pants. Wiping his chest and legs best he could with a dry towel, he found a clean shirt and a new pair of pants, put them on.

In the kitchen he washed his face. Suddenly he felt very tired.

There was a bucket under the sink and he took this. The sink had a spray nozzle at the end of a piece of retractable tubing and he tore this tubing out and then broke the spray nozzle off, leaving water gouting up in the sink. He coiled the tubing, dropping it into the bucket.

Gous was awake now in the bedroom, groggy, rubbing his head.

"You shouldn't do this," he said.

"Nothing personal," said Kline. "You'll thank me for it later," he said, and then struck Gous again, this time on the side of his head.

He searched Gous, taking his cigarette lighter. Gous' car keys and wallet he threw out the window, and then he left.

V.

He stayed there, leaning his head against the steering wheel. *Is there any other choice?* he was wondering. The plastic of the steering wheel was slick and cold.

Of course there's another choice, he thought. *There is always another choice. I'm just not going to take it.*

He lifted his head. On the seat beside him, a collection of objects, disjecta: a bucket, a coil of tubing, a cigarette lighter, a cleaver, a pistol, a man's head.

He lifted the head by the hair and dumped it into the bucket, the tubing as well. The cigarette lighter he forced into a pocket. The gun he slid into his belt, the cleaver as well.

He got out carrying the bucket, then set it down on the curb, taking the head and the tubing out.

He snaked one end of the tubing into the car's gas tank and sucked on the other end, feeling the rough plastic of the broken nozzle with his tongue until gas poured first into his mouth and then onto the sidewalk and then into the bucket. He let the bucket fill about three quarters full, then pulled the tube free, threw it under the car.

He carried the sloshing bucket a few dozen meters down the sidewalk. He stopped just shy of the revolving door, and left it there against the building wall.

It's not too late, he thought on his way back for the head, but knew it was—even before he'd picked up the head, even before he'd carried it through the revolving doors and into the lobby.

The doorman Paul was there, or a doorman Paul anyway. How had the sequence gone?

"Well met, Paul," said Kline.

"Well met, Paul," said the Paul. "Friend Kline, I mean."

"Just have to report," said Kline.

"Of course," said the Paul. "Might I ask what you have in your hand?"

"This?" said Kline. "Borchert's head."

"Ah, I see," said the Paul.

"I'm going to put him down," said Kline. "I left something outside."

The Paul nodded, started toward the desk and the telephone. Kline hurried outside, took the bucket by the handle, carried it sloshing back in.

By the time he returned, the Paul was already unlocking the heavy door. Kline came closer and put down the bucket and waited.

"You know where to find him," the Paul said. "He'll be waiting for you," he said, and reached out to open the door. Whereupon Kline killed him with the cleaver.

There was a Paul on the other side of the door and Kline greeted him and killed him as well. This Paul was a little harder to kill, having caught a glimpse of the first guard prone on the floor just before Kline swung the cleaver, but in the end he was dead too.

He dragged in the bucket of gasoline, sliding Borchert's head along with his foot.

From there it was just a matter of dousing the parquet and the walls. He spread some in the entryway and then up the stairs and down the hall at the top of the stairs as well. Then he went back down, lighting it as he went.

By the time he reached the bottom, Borchert's head was a ball of fire and there were blue flames licking the floor and walls and Kline's hand was blistering. His shoes and legs and shirt were aflame. He tried to beat himself out and when it kept up he pushed his way out the door and rolled in the doorman's blood. And then, still smoking, his hands starting to shake, he took the doorman's keys and stood at the door, watching. Once he heard shouts, he closed the door, and locked it.

He stood beside the door, listening to what might be screams, what might be merely the crackle and roar of the flames. When it grew too hot and the door itself began to smoke he moved back and slowly away until finally he was standing alone in the street, watching the entire building catch fire. He listened to the sound of the sirens, distant but coming closer.

Where now? he wondered, at first walking, then loping, then breaking into a run. *What next?*

ACKNOWLEDGMENTS

Thanks are due to Paul Miller for first publishing "The Brotherhood of Mutilation" and Paul DiFilippo for writing an introduction to that volume. I'd also like to thank Paul Maliszewski and Paul Tobin Anderson for advice concerning one-handed piano performances and for putting me on the trail of Paul Wittgenstein, the one-armed pianist (and brother of Ludwig Wittgenstein), and Paul LaFarge and Forrest Paul Gander for general encouragement. And to my girlfriend, Paul, and to my two daughters, Paul and Paul.

And the greatest thanks to three honorary Pauls—my publisher Victoria Blake, my agent Matt McGowan, my French editor Claro— and to the ever-generous and ever-brilliant Peter Straub.

ABOUT THE AUTHOR

Brian Evenson is the author of nine books of fiction, including *The Open Curtain* (2006), which was a finalist for the International Horror Guild Award and the Edgar Award and was named one of the ten best books of the year by *Time Out New York*. Evenson's most recent collection of stories, *The Wavering Knife* (2004), won the International Horror Guild Award. Among his other books are *Altmann's Tongue* (1994), which was the cause of a great deal of controversy, leading to his leaving a teaching job at Mormon-owned Brigham Young University and to his eventual break with the Mormon Church. In 2008 he published *Aliens: No Exit*, an *Alien* movie tie-in novel, from DH Press. A new story collection, *Fugue State*, will be published by Coffee House Press in 2009. He has also published a critical study of novelist Robert Coover and several book-length translations from French, and he is an occasional collaborator with graphic novelist Zak Sally. Evenson's work has been translated into French, Spanish, Italian, and Japanese. He directs Brown University's Creative Writing Program and lives in Providence, Rhode Island with writer Joanna Howard and their dog Ruby. You can find out more about his work at www.brianevenson.com.

ABOUT THE BOOK

Last Days began its life in 2002, when Paul Miller of Earthling Publications approached Brian Evenson about writing a limited-edition novella. At the time, Evenson had just read *Red Harvest* and was fascinated by Dashiell Hammett's relentlessness. He had rediscovered Philip K. Dick's *A Scanner Darkly*, and loved how Dick grafted noir to science fiction. Then he stumbled onto Jonathan Lethem's *Gun, with Occasional Music*, re-read Peter Straub's beautifully crafted *The Throat*, and started looking at Joel-Peter Witkin's photographs. With all that whirling in his head, he sat down, had a few false starts, but eventually arrived at the idea for "The Brotherhood of Mutilation." Earthling published the book, and very quickly it sold out.

Everybody thought that was the end of the project. But somehow a few prints of the original 315-copy print run of the novella got into the right hands. One went to Claro, the French editor of a series called Lot 49, who decided to publish it in translation. Another made its way to Denmark, to the filmmaker Karim Ghahwagi, who wrote a screenplay. Another went to Victoria Blake, then an editor at DH Press, the prose division of Dark Horse Comics.

Almost immediately after the initial publication, Evenson wanted to continue the story, but he knew it needed to hold its own against "The Brotherhood." He was still reading noirs—work by Fredrick Brown, Dan Marlowe, David Goodis, and Richard Stark was most important. Then he saw Odd Nerdrum's painting *One Story Singer*. When two friends separately mentioned that Ludwig Wittgenstein's brother Paul was a one-handed piano player, the elements of "Last Days" suddenly fell into place. By that time, Victoria Blake had started Underland Press, and wanted to publish both of the novellas as a single novel. The first edition was published as an original trade paperback in February 2009.